Murder at Osgoode Hall

An Amicus Curiae Mystery

Published by ECW PRESS
2120 Queen Street East, Suite 200, Toronto, Ontario, Canada M4E 1E2

NATIONAL LIBRARY OF CANADA CATALOGUING IN PUBLICATION

Miller, Jeffrey, 1950
Murder at Osgoode Hall / Jeffrey Miller.
(An Amicus Curiae mystery)

ISBN 1-55022-635-5

1. Title. II. Series: Miller, Jeffrey, 1950– . Amicus Curiae mystery.

PS8626.I45M87 2004   C813'.6   C2003-907290-8

Cover and Text Design: Tania Craan
Cover illustration: Gordon Sauve
Production and Typesetting: Mary Bowness
Printing: Gauvin Press

This book is set in Solstice and Garamond.

The publication of *Murder at Osgoode Hall* has been generously supported by the Canada Council, the Ontario Arts Council, the Ontario Media Development Corporation, and the Government of Canada through the Book Publishing Industry Development Program. **Canadä**

DISTRIBUTION
CANADA: Jaguar Book Group, 100 Armstrong Avenue, Georgetown, ON, L7G 5S4

UNITED STATES: Independent Publishers Group, 814 North Franklin Street, Chicago, Illinois 60610

PRINTED AND BOUND IN CANADA

ECW PRESS
ecwpress.com

Murder at Osgoode Hall

An Amicus Curiae Mystery

JEFFREY MILLER

ECW PRESS

"For I have heard . . . the voice of the daughter of Zion, that bewaileth herself, that spreadeth her hands, saying, Woe is me now! for my soul is wearied because of murderers." Jeremiah IV, 31

FOR JACK DAVID, BEST FRIEND TO WAIFS AND STRAYS

The law, setting, and forensic science in this novel are meant to be as accurate as a tall tale permits, and real controversies at the Law Society of Upper Canada have provided its inspiration. However, the characters and events are completely fictional. I am fortunate to have many friends at Osgoode Hall, including benchers on both sides of the big firm-little firm controversies, and I mean to keep them.

Very small bits of Chapters Four and Five of Part Two appeared previously, in entirely different contexts, in *The Lawyers Weekly*, and Sir Robert Megarry is the source of the contempt case I mention in Part Two, Chapter Six. Both the signs described in Chapter Two, Part Two are real, although I saw the one about the master of the universe not in Toronto but outside the Divine Light Mission in Boulder, Colorado about 30 years ago. The DNA evidence in the Beamish murder case is in fact discussed in the edition of *Nature* specified in Chapter Two of Part Two, and Amicus's legal history of the cat in Part Two is drawn from reputable, albeit human, sources.

Jeffrey Miller
January, 2004

CONTENTS

PART ONE

In Mercy

To be in or commended to mercy:
"In criminal law, the discretion of a judge
. . . to remit altogether the punishment to
which a convicted person is liable, or to
mitigate the severity of his sentence."
Black's Law Dictionary, fifth edition

CHAPTER 1

A Friend of the Court

Oh, yes, absolutely: Osgoode Hall is the perfect place for murder. A hundred and forty years of renovation, titivation, extravagation, that's what's done it. In the end, all that high-mindedness has created more shadow than light. Like history itself, the Hall, built originally to house the province's highest courts, is defined by the dark corners and dead ends that shape all mortal delusions of grandeur. It's pretty enough, in its vainglorious and titivating-in-the-looking-glass way; deceptively beautiful, even: garish with catwalks, ramps, winding and grand-carpeted staircases, but also those dim'n'dreary, mostly deserted and dead-straight concrete-and-lino utilitarian back steps down which you can break your head and neck; balustrades, aged galleria and pediments (indoors and out) over which to plummet-plunge-dive and shatter your spine, or from which to hang by your windpipe 'til ye be dead, dead, and dissected; ancient ovens and stoves and chimneys and boilers whose decrepit valves and liners threaten at any moment to hiss forth deadly fumes or scalding slurry; massive chandeliers and clocks on the manor-house scale to come crashing down on your unsuspecting brains; overused and disused two-storey stepladders to splayleg-collapse-crumble under you as you *stretch, stretch, grasp* at aged statute books and court records whose guts disintegrate in rusty gusts amid your fingers, history's, *entropy's* dust blinding and choking you *(hack hack)* as you struggle for your footing and bark your shins before shattering your skeleton on the floor; not to mention, *pant pant* (and here endeth, you will be relieved to learn, the First Architectural Lesson) obscure library stacks where the photocopy machines hum away all bored and innocent, alone and lonely in the shadows, standing patiently by to French-fry the innards of the odd Law Society bencher.

But that particular homicide comes later in this chronicle. The murder immediately "at bar," as we like to say here at the home of the Court of Appeal, "may be dealt with more briefly." I quote that favourite phrase from His Lordship Theodore Elisha Mariner, Justice of Appeal (Old Ted to his cronies), the very man who now sits in final judgment of Yours Now and Then Truly — or, rather, at this very moment His Lordship stands all red-faced and judgmental over me as the alleged victim droops lifelessly in my mouth.

Ya got me bang to rights guv'nor.

From his office window overlooking Queen Street West, Mr. Justice Mariner takes a personal interest in Osgoode's park-like grounds. He has donated a stand of apricot trees, personally cultivated in his garden in upper Forest Hill Village and transplanted to Osgoode Hall about four years ago — saplings which remain leafless, "bare ruin'd choirs where late the sweet dinner-birds sang" on this late-February morning. Apparently His Lordship had also developed a special fondness for a pair of cardinals frequenting one of the aged maples on the grounds, inseparable mates who subsisted through the dour Canadian winter on crusts of bread and muffin, or on seeds scattered by visitors or (more likely) by loiterers and the assorted homeless persons who frequent the environs of Osgoode and the nearby City Halls, Old and New. I fear, in other words, that this was one of those cases in which the court itself constituted judge, jury, prosecutor, and, alas, eyewitness for the prosecution. The court was sitting — or standing — *ex proprio motu*, as His Lordship might say, on its own motion. And judgment was summarily severe.

Perhaps it would be convenient to add at this juncture that your occasionally faithful correspondent, the accused at bar, serves his life's sentence in the species *felis sylvestris*, laterally known as *felis catus*, an uncommon and not altogether domesticated, yes, you've got it in one, four-legged C-A-T, appropriately dressed for the high judicial occasion in my finest robe of silken black cat's fur and two whiter-than-white fleecy tabs, as we call them at Osgoode Hall, running at a forty-five-degree angle to one another down my black-coated chest from their intersection at the base of my throat. I appear, in other words, fully robed for the occasion, given that I am so dressed, naturally, for all occasions. (That's *tabs*, by the way, not *tabby*.) Caught red-handed — or dripping red-mawed, for it was the bleeding male cardinal between my needle-tipped canines *(canines? I ask you, canines?)* — I do what any self-respecting villain does in such circumstances. As the deceased lolls casually in my mouth, I fix my impenetrable gaze on His Lordship's gimlet eye and I cry: *I didn't do it, Me Lud, honest.*

Mr. Justice Mariner is having none of it, of course, never mind that I enjoy a complete defence of necessity at natural law. All I was doing, after all, was getting my living in the way nature intended. As a weekend naturalist, the court should appreciate this. At worst, Yours Ferally is guilty of hunting without a licence — a licence granted outside human jurisdiction, considering that the Law of Nature gives me all the licence I need. (Consider: What humanity views as feline indifference to its rules is in fact a legitimate argument against your self-declared right to despoil the planet according to your selfish whim.) *What was my client's alternative, My Lord, starvation? As the law says of the prisoner who breaks out of a burning jailhouse, am I to be hanged because I would not stay to be burnt?*

Just outside the cow gates separating the Hall from the pavement on University Avenue, I can hear the Voice of Doom, as Osgoode's habitués call old Ernie, the street evangelist, with his electronic megaphone. *Were they ashamed-a, when they had committed abomination-a? Nay, they were not at all ashamed-a. Neither could they blush-a. Therefore they shall fall among them that fall-a. At the time that I visit them-a they shall be cast down-a, saith the Lord. Repent, saith the Lord. Repent-a!*

In lieu of a black cap, the judge puts his hand over the top of his greying noggin, sighs, grunts, scowls, shakes said noggin and pronounces sentence of death: "Bury the poor bird under the apricot trees, if the ground's not too hard, and take this verminous murderer down to the Humane Society."

Take him down, bailiff!

A broadsheet section of the *Globe and Mail* scuds along the sidewalk and catches in the iron fencing. *Dead cat walking!* But immediately from the well of the court, or at least from the clot of lollygagging Oz Hall employees, semi-resident homeless persons, and passing John and Jane Does in the late-winter courtyard, there is an appeal. Spring is in the air. A friend of the court, the perfect combination of the "reasonable person" and "officious bystander" you find perambulating helpfully through the caselaw reports (to be used as a benchmark for the litigants' conduct) comes to life right there on the courthouse grounds, sips at her paper cup of milky tea, then pipes up: "That's not necessary, Ted. We can look after him. We can keep him in the library. He'll control the other vermin there — at least of the four-footed variety."

The Lord is thy shepherd-a.

"I don't think so, Katrina," His Lordship says, shaking his head grimly amidst the applause and other seconding motions. *Be thou instructed, O Jerusalem-a, lest my soul depart from thee-a; lest I make thee desolate-a, a land not inhabited.* "To begin with, the benchers wouldn't like it."

The court's friend and my prospective angel of mercy is none other than Katrina Slovenskaya, assistant librarian in the Great Library, through the main doors, up the grand staircase to the second floor south. (And the benchers, as my readers might well know, are Law Society officials elected by its member lawyers to help regulate the profession and run its daily affairs, including those of the library.) Truth be told, Katrina has shared her tuna, salmon-salad, or Cheez Whiz sandwich and milky tea with me and other feline denizens of the Hall during more than one al fresco fair-weather luncheon. But she does not share that particular tidbit of evidence with the Court just now.

"If it's a *fait accompli*, what can they say?" she asks, smiling but red-faced in the cold. Her bulbous little nose glows positively crimson, set off against the bloodless white in the smile wrinkles around it. Though she is in her forties, I imagine, she looks rather like someone's little Russian grandma, or at least maiden auntie.

"The quality of mercy is not strained, particularly if the old fuss-budgets don't know about it," she admonishes the judge, quoting his favourite author, it turns out. *Translation: Ignorance is bliss.*

The Court scowls again *(Repent-a!)*, removes his hand from his head and taps Yours Now and Then Sincerely with the tip of his judicial boot as I hang my head in mock shame and drop the deceased on the cold, hard, still miserably hibernating earth. Showing remorse is *de rigueur*, after all, when you're speaking to sentence, particularly in capital cases, even for *felis sylvestris*. "Just keep him out of the garden for the time being, then. He's on bail pending my deliberations as to sentence. But I want to make one thing crystal clear, Katrina: Any breach of conditions will result in the most serious sanction, and his immediate removal from civilian life." *Repent-a!* His Lordship sets his chin at us as though he is banging down a gavel on his high-rise bench.

When the judge has left *(appeal allowed!)* and Katrina has gathered me to her capacious bosom, she asks the lissom lady standing next to her, her colleague Elise Throckmorton, research librarian and as willowy as Katrina is plump, a reverse shadow, pallid and delicate from all those dusty, bookish hours out of the sun:

"What shall we call him, then?"

"I don't know," Elise answers. "What about Amicus? You know, as in *amicus curiae*, 'friend of the court'?"

"Amicus," Katrina says to Yours Intermittently Faithful, almost squeezing the just-rescued eighth or ninth life out of me. "Amicus of Osgoode, Q.C. — Questing Cat." Katrina nearly smothers me in her lavender-water glee, the two of them giggling like schoolgirls and mauling Yours Questingly (I ask you!) in open public view. To ease her grip, and concurrently ingratiate myself further into the court's mercy, I rub my head this way and that against her cherubic chin and let the blood thrum through the old thorax so that the susceptible can hear it as an almost subsonic ululation, a love call and aural narcotic all at once — *pur-r-r-r-rur-rur, pur-r-r-r-rur pur-r-r-rur. . . . Ronronner,* I believe the French call it. *Le mot juste,* and as nature's gypsy in an officially bilingual state, I reserve the right to use it. *Ronronner, ronronner, ronronner,* I add officiously bilingually to the conversation on the Hall's lawn.

Apparently, though, this is a Latin occasion.

"Amicus," Elise Throckmorton says, and scratches me behind my black silken ears. "Amicus of Osgoode Hall, Q.C."

. . . I am become a name;
For always roaming with a hungry heart
Much have I seen and known.

"Amicus," Katrina Slovenskaya answers, and *(ronronner, ronronner, ronronner)* we head for the oak doors at the main entryway, just in time for a second cup of tea.

The conditions of my bail, as imposed by Mr. Justice Mariner, include, in his memorable phrase, "Make sure the little bugger gets the snip." It is, I must say, a redundant precaution. Alas, the outward manifestations of my masculinity were snatched from me some time ago, during my last stint in Her Majesty's Doghouse on River Street, aka the Toronto Inhumane Society's so-called shelter. (So as not to offend anyone's sensibilities, and in the modern spirit of calling a spade a manual excavating implement, your governments have taken to calling prisons "correctional centres and institutions." In that same spirit, you will understand that I do not call this particular institution "Her Majesty's Cathouse.") And they wonder why male cats are stand-offish and aggressive. Mind you, it's funny to begin with that they say domestic felines are aloof. No amount of bravado or pride can change the fact that compromise rules our lives. It's a matter of survival.

Still, like many of my ilk, I have been a rambling man, now and again wild and footloose, roaming with a hungry heart when that urge for going blinds and deafens one to all else. Then, one morning, you find yourself heartsick of hunting, and scrapping, begging and fornicating and dodging, and you yearn almost as keenly for the quiet life at the hearth. There is that other, shrewder, more gnawing hunger, for peace and security. So you find it, if you can. And of course the older you get, the closer the balance moves toward weighing up evenly between the itchy feet and grumbling belly.

So for now, *I am become a name*, momentarily sated with roaming in my hungry heart, ordained by circumstance to my task,

by slow prudence to make mild
a rugged people [these rude denizens of Osgoode Hall]
and through soft degrees
Subdue them to the useful and the good.

I am Amicus of Osgoode Hall, where, before long, it is just-spring and Osgoode Hall is mud-yucch-ish and puddle-awful. And Mr. Justice Mariner is working on an Important Paper. I know, because I have just sat on the draft of pages eight and nine while he was trying to work on them in his office. Twisting my head catlike down and to the left while pretending to groom the general region of my left clavicle, I am able to see the title page, too, because it sticks out from the pile seven pages south of page eight: "Environmentalist Protesters and the *Public Lands Act*: Reasonable Limits on the 'Reasonable Limits' We Impose on Free Expression and Mobility Rights." Sighing, but more or less thankfully distracted from his analysis of the common law of trespass versus constitutional guarantees of free expression and movement, His Lordship wanders to the window. A battalion of black attack squirrels earnestly strips the green apricot fruitlings from his trees in Osgoode's front courtyard. The fruit has only just begun to set, and the trees' white blossoms litter the not-quite-green lawn like a late flurry of vegetable snow. The windows being caulked shut, the Court gallops out of his office door and down the back stairways, in danger of tripping on his robes, which he has only just put on for the afternoon sitting in the Court of Appeal. *I didn't do it, guv'nor, honest,* I note, ambling to the self-same window where late His Lordship groaned. Eventually I see the ancient Mariner spin his way like a nun in full habit, but not without agility, through the angled iron cow gate at the City Hall end of the grounds. Then the old salt sprints at full quintagenarian tilt toward said tree-stand, waving his berobed arms like black crow's wings and skrikering very injudiciously at said outsized rodents.

Babbleybabbleybabble! Babbleybabbleybabble! says he; or at least so it sounds from two storeys up. So much for free expression among tree-huggers.

Soon he brings back with him hard evidence of the crime, fairly weeping over it, shaking his head and sighing like a mourner. He shows Exhibits One and One-A to Yours Semi-Domestically: two neatly broken halves of a baby apricot. "On top of everything else, they're not even eating the damn fruit," he cries. "Just the kernel. Just the useless damn pit." I glance out the window, and sure enough, dozens, perhaps hundreds, of baby apricot halves litter the awakening lawn. No doubt the squirrels pleaded necessity, just as I had done before the Court.

"You know, he looks sort of like one of those black velvet paintings, doesn't he?" Elise Throckmorton says. "If you ignore those white stripes on his chest, of course." The library has only just opened on this warm April morning, and Elise is taking her turn in what my Great Librarians call the Duck Blind, the desk where they are almost hidden by the cubicle dividers but are betrayed by a fancy little brass sign that says *Reference Librarian*. Before the library's most recent and most extravagant renovation, apparently the Duck Blind was truly a lonely and not very obscure spot, set out in the middle of the Reference Room, just asking for trouble. Now its inhabitant potshots reference questions while situated to the side, behind attractive polyethylene panelling, adjacent to the desk of Ms. Katrina Slovenskaya, which worthy answers Elise: "Not as much as my Mingus at home," meaning, of course, that I don't look as much like a black velvet kitten as her Mingus does, which is just as well, as far as I and black velvet paintings are concerned.

Katrina has two Humane Society moggies *chez elle*, Grimalkin (so called after the witch's cat in *Macbeth)*, a mostly Russian Blue, judging by the photos on Katrina's desk, and, yes, her Mingus, Black Like Me yet without the barrister's tabs down the chest. But then, he's named after the jazz bassist, who I understand to have been a taciturn bruiser with very little resemblance to black velvet paintings of kittens.

Mind you, one can be rather too literal, or at least altogether unsentimental, in naming household pets. Just before the so-called Animal Rescue snatched Yours Vagrantly off the streets and so rudely maimed me in my tomhood at the Big House, I was the more or less welcome border and resident mouser at Levy's Delicatessen, in Kensington Market. The Levys were *sympathique* but not at all sentimental. They called me Katz (Cat), or Ketz, rather, which they seemed to think was the English translation. When they were in a good mood, I was Ketzl or Ketzeleh — Kitten, Little Cat. But their home was not mine. Before locking up the store each night and during Jewish holidays, Mr. Levy would waggle his finger at me and say, "Now I doan vant you making no mess in mine store, here, you, Ketz. I doan vant you should sit on your *tuchis* the mice is eating on mine inventory, you. No, no, no. I'm telling you, you don't make nice, you shot, you, Ketz," by which I assume he meant fired. He was not, after all, a violent man. If the holiday was for more than a day, he would add, "Now you pay attention you should gobble that foods here too fast, you. I'm putting you here foods, you make this last for you the two days, you, Ketzl, before I'm coming back in here."

Then there was the day they didn't come in there at all. Old man Levy died one cold January morning when he went out to warm up the car to drive himself and the old lady to the store. Or so I overheard from the real estate agent. In the interim I survived quite nicely by methodically cleaning out the deli's cheese and meat counters, the smorgasbord of the garbage-picker's dreams. Or, as Mr. Levy liked to tell his customers (may he rest in peace), "The tastiest fish is from somebody else's table."

My lease, as it were, was extended when two college drop-outs bought the place and turned it into one of your trendier eat-in delis. But not more than a year later they sold it to a balding and nasty stump of humanity who chewed dead cigar ends in his brown and broken teeth, his thick arms brushing his barrel chest with every brutal little step as he marched robotically around the stripped-down store, marking everything with the insult of his body odour — a septic Napoleon, he was, his eyes hard with the purblindness of those who have only half a soul (the half which looks inward only), choking on his own selfish misery as he lashed out at whichever employee, family member, or companion animal happened to be within bullying range. The old deli became a rummy-and-drifter's bar, further depressed by derelict, stoned-out rock bands and, sometimes, strippers.

Napoleon's lost "girls" were stereotypically solicitous enough — stroking and fussing over me dreamily as we clucked about our aromatic little patron, whom we could only pity. Attempting to insinuate my sympathy into his pinched universe, sinuously stroking his legs with my silken coat, back and forth, forth and back, back and forth, convinced this would help him find his inner child, I got his size 7-½ up my backside instead. Instinctively I raked his greasy shin, sockless in its torn deck shoe, from just below his fat knee down across the top of his lipidinous foot. The four burgeoning stripes of red amidst the dirt and sweat and wiry hair left the bizarre impression that he was wearing one of the girls' fishnet stockings. He swung the bleeding appendage at me again, but I was long gone — out to Queen Street once more, and not long after, solitary confinement, aka "Intake Quarantine," at the Inhumane Society on River.

Then it was a brief stint as Muffy in a Victorian semi-detached on Spruce Street, near Gerrard and Parliament. Before long domestication went stale again and the semi-wild funk of the city streets was back in my nostrils, and back in my blood, so I hot-footed it, until I landed anew in the River Street Doghouse, only to be rescued and abandoned once more. And then, as you have witnessed, it was the Hall and environs, ever and always at the peripatetically tender mercies of *Homo allegedly sapiens* — H.A.S. or Has-beings for short, as our feline scholars call your two-footed, narcissistic species. So really, it should be Katz of Osgoode Hall, I guess, pending an application under the *Change of Name* and *Identification of Criminals Acts.*

Which all goes to show that sometimes "black velvet kitten" is in the eye of the beholder. At Elise Throckmorton's comparison of my noble self to such emetic eructions of the vulgar sentiment, I leap from the edge of the Duck Blind, nearly toppling a large and fully gowned barrister just arriving all in a huff-and-pant, desperate to know, before court starts in precisely 48 minutes, how to establish the priority of the third mortgage held by his client, a Saudi Arabian investor, judging from the papers that scatter all over the floor as the lawyer tries not to trip over Yours Acrobatically and catapult into the Duck Blind on top of our pre-Raphaelite Ms. Throckmorton. As the lawyer recovers himself and steps over me, grunting and looming as he gathers his precious documents, I scoot off for the Journals Room one floor below — where, as I say, I am to make a most shocking discovery.

CHAPTER 2

The Splinter

His name was Jeremiah "The Splinter" Debeers, and, though he was 46 years old or so, he still lived with his mother, in a condominium in the city's arid north end. Or at least he had been ordinarily resident there, as we barristers and solicitors say, until a few hours previous. He earned the sobriquet "the splintered bencher" very early in his career as an official at the Law Society, where it took him less than a month to become a pain in the backsides of his colleagues, going off loudly and publicly on his own anti-Establishment crusades — splintering painfully off, in other words. Some blamed his obscure religious fundamentalism — no one was sure of what brand; Dutch Calvinist, perhaps, or Baptist, or Presbyterian, maybe even not-exactly-Christian. Others speculated that he was dominated by his scraggly-scrappy immigrant mother. Whatever explained it, while he socialized amicably enough and even cracked the occasional smile, he was never known to swear or drink alcohol, coffee, or tea, and he was resolutely unavailable for any Sunday function.

Some of the other benchers — oaken, smooth-sanded pillars of the profession that they were — wondered aloud why Jerry the Splinter bothered to run for bencher in the first place, taking time from his practice to suffer through forty or sixty hours worth of mind-numbing meetings per month, fussing and fuming over budgets and professional regulation and libraries and professional competence and public relations, not to mention the never-ending round of stale finger-sandwich functions and rubber-chicken-and-plonk dinners (not that, as vegetarian teetotaller, Jerry Debeers partook of much of the fare), the endless calls to the bar of freshly minted barristers and solicitors and future benchers. . . . Why bother with all of that when he professed such derision for the whole enterprise? But on second thought, his colleagues admitted that the answer was obvious. Being contrarian was Jerry Debeers' thing, his way of distinguishing himself in the profession — a profession of Establishment conformists — of standing out not at the bar, but well behind it, waiting in ambush for his less fastidious colleagues. Somebody had to do it, so why not a lonely, middle-aged man who lived with his mother?

And now, like a snitch in the alley, he lies dead, sprawled motionless on his right side, a crazy-legged trapezoid of flesh and synthetic textiles, just in front and partly to the right of the photocopier in the Journals Room. *Dead.* (I walk gingerly to the left of his corpse, sniffing, pawing, poking, gingerly, tenderly, recoiling as he seems to move; sniffing, pawing, poking, recoiling). *Alive?* No. *Deader* (doubly-gingerly, poke-about, poke-about, sniff, poke-about, to the right). *Deadest* (for ultimate measure, I tiptoe up his hip and onto his shoulder, take a good whiff right left centre right, before sticking my muzzle in his left ear and then up the complementary nostril. *Ack! Sneeze! Ack!*). Burnt cotton, singed wool and rayon *whew-sneeze-ack!* (his off-the-rack plaid jacket, no doubt, and a striped tie of plasticized fabric), and, not to put too fine a point on it, cooked flesh, tissue, viscera. Boiled blood. Black puddin'. Oh, my.

Thou wretched rash intruding fool, farewell. I took thee for thy better.

There is not much in the way of gore, mind you — which would little trouble one practised in the eviscerating arts, anyway, of course — none, in fact, that I can detect with any of my senses. But the stench of entropy overwhelms — rotting paper and library glue and flesh, and furniture polish and Windex and floor wax, commingled in close quarters with that *soupçon* of burnt tissue. It is all emetic enough that, drawing the whiskers back on my snout and sneezing again ever so slightly, I am about to skedaddle for the main stacks when my saviour Katrina Slovenskaya arrives with the barrister of the Saudi Arabian mortgage problem, and they catch me out with my forepaws on the deceased bencher's lifeless rib cage. Katrina brings her plump little hand to her plumply heaving bosom and she says, quietly, quietly, "Oh my God," to which I reply, in sincerest honesty this time, looking up slowly at Katrina, all wide-eyed innocence and good faith:

I didn't do it, m'Lady, honest.

As far as Samuel Fitz-Niblick, Q.C., was concerned, Jerry Debeers stood charged with what *Reader's Digest* used to call more picturesque speech. Fitz-Niblick was less than impressed, if occasionally amused, by Debeers' propensity for long-winded tirades, rarely on point, during convocation and committee meetings. Then there was his habit of running to the press to report in excruciating detail how his fellow benchers favoured the big downtown law firms, all the while feasting at the fatted calf of membership dues paid by less fortunate barristers and solicitors. "My false prophet colleagues," Debeers habitually called his bencher peers, "who gorge themselves upon the fleshpots of Egypt." For good measure he published his own newsletter — called, what else?, *Jeremiad* and available free on his Internet website — to chronicle the latest outrage at the Society.

It was widely said, Fitz-Niblick knew, that Debeers had the time, leisure, and sour grapes for such bitterness because his own practice was just about non-existent, never mind the steady supply of dodgy professionals he prosecuted in professional discipline proceedings at the College of Physicians and Surgeons, Teachers' College, Ontario Securities Commission, and so on (Jeremiah Debeers not only talked the holier-than-thou talk, he walked the walk, at least when he could get a prosecution file from this or that discipline committee), and never mind the persistently hot market for Toronto real estate, his long-standing legal speciality.

The sale-of-land game was where Jerry had started out, in fact, selling houses and strip mall leaseholds for Heap-o-Livin' Real Estate. In his thirties, after seeing how lawyers grew wealthy on land transfers without having to drive all over "Heck and back at all hours the good Lord sends," he went to law school. His mother subsidized him his legal training and never let him forget it, apparently, even after he had set himself up in his one-man real estate law practice, using the contacts he had made as a salesman.

If pressed on the subject in his official capacity as Law Society

Treasurer (head of the benchers and the society), Sammy Fitz-Niblick would admit that he often wished on the evening's first star that Jerry Debeers would come to appreciate that he was spitting in the communal soup. And after one particularly nerve-wracking convocation, as the bencher's call their official meetings, I myself heard the treasurer ask (winking broadly at his colleagues), "Hey, Jer, how's the real estate bar like a bucket of take-out chicken?"

Debeers dryly replied: "Yeah, I know, Sammy. It's all right wings and backsides. Very funny, just like it was the first time I heard it, twenty years ago."

"Actually, I would have said right wings and *arseholes*," Fitz-Niblick muttered to Roman Nobb, Q.C., who sat next to him in the benchers' dining room. The two Queen's Counsel were known to pal around, I had discovered, and just the sight of them entering a room made people smile. Both cultivated an air of elegance and charm, the art of the shmooze, but that wasn't exactly what bemused about them. Fitz-Niblick was a short, balding, roly-poly immigrant from Jamaica who had to try much harder than Roman Nobb. The treasurer was the colour of light-roast coffee, with tufts of silvery hair billowing around his ears and at his thatch-like eyebrows. Nobb was as close to aristocratic as you can get in Canada, coming from an old Toronto family, his father having served as the province's Chief Justice and in the Canadian senate. Nobb towered over the little Jamaican, tall and handsome, with a full head of silver hair, never mind that, like Fitz-Niblick, he was in his sixties. He still carried himself like he was the most popular boy at Upper Canada College. Together, the two benchers looked a little like a comedy act, to the point that the grimmest cynics whispered it was a conspiracy — that their friendship was all about politics and calculation, another way that they jollied everyone else they dealt with into their greedy clutches. And from what I could tell, there might have been something to this. Unfortunately, as Nobb was a little deaf, Fitz-Niblick had to repeat himself, *miu forte*: "I said I would have used the phrase right wings and *arseholes*."

"Which means you're fifty per cent qualified, doesn't it, Rolly?" Debeers' best, and as far as was known, only friend, Josey Probert, another Toronto bencher — like Debeers, from the northern suburbs — piped in at that point, arching both eyebrows.

But over time Fitz-Niblick seemed to have grown sanguine about Debeers. *Let he who is without sin. . . .* At least publicly, Fitz-Niblick long ago had stopped reacting to the Splinter with anything more than a bemused smile. True enough, and as some of the benchers felt compelled to confess to the police, he played along with the running joke that had developed at bencher meetings where Debeers was not physically present, a game that put forward various sordid and gruesome ways of doing the Splinter in, the more graphic the better.

"It'd be easy enough," someone would say at one or another confab or booze-up, "to get him to tumble ass over tea-kettle down one of the stairways we're always huffing and puffing around in this old place."

"Especially with wet shoes in the dead of our endless winter," someone else would dryly reply, munching gaily on a triangle of toast with smoked salmon, goat's cheese, and desiccated black olive.

"Or with that bloody cat running all over the place under foot when you don't expect it," Nobb, it was, added on one especially memorable occasion, sipping at his single malt from the Law

Society's cellar. "Bugger darted right in front of me going down the staircase from the library yesterday."

Ya got me bang to rights, guv'nor. I admit it: there's something about the old snob that rubs me the wrong way, as it were.

Mind you, who could blame them, really? Occasionally one had to talk about something other than capping the number of new lawyers admitted to the bar, how to reduce the premiums on malpractice insurance, the newest stratagem for wresting back control of legal aid from the government, and, most pointedly, whether to serve caviar or foie gras at this year's Christmas party.

"Maybe we could sic that seedy old moggy on Jerry in particular. Mind you, I've slipped down one of those bookshelf ladders in the library, myself — in high heels, though, and while I was juggling four volumes of the *Statutes of New Brunswick*," someone else would have put in, giggling and sipping coffee out of the white china service emblazoned with the Society emblem, with its "two stags trippant" and a beaver carrying a sprig of maple leaves in its jaws as Hercules and sword-wielding Justice look on.

Anyway, as I say, Osgoode Hall is the perfect place for murder mysteries, and for plotting them — murders to the manor born, as it were. Not that the Splinter was often absent from meetings of the committees on which he sat; but even a gadfly of his magnitude could not serve and protect everywhere, all the time. He had that moribund law practice to run, of course, barely scraping by, it seemed, partly because he was so busy being the official sliver in the Law Society's behind. In his absence, anyway, and on a stroll through the monthly meeting of the Standing Committee on Professional Competence, I heard one of his colleagues, Mr. Nobb, it well could have been again, suggest that it would not be murder if someone were "to poke Debeers up the arse some cloudy spring morning with a poisoned umbrella tip, say. Provocation reduces murder to manslaughter, doesn't it, Sammy, if I remember my first-year Criminal?"

"Hell, you'd be acquitted altogether, my friend," Fitz-Niblick replied, waving a glass of something vaguely yellow and bubbly. "Self-defence. Hell, defence of necessity, man." Then, ham that he famously was, he put on his most dramatic evangelist's voice: "False prophets must be annihilated in Gawd's name!"

"You mean like how they assassinated that Hungarian diplomat or whatever he was," Eleanor Rorschach-Bulwark, bencher for the southwestern region, said, "in the 1970s, I think it was?"

"It wasn't an umbrella tip, actually. They shot this little pellet out of a hole in the tip." This would have been Dylan Faddaster, know-it-all about town and, in his spare time from that, legal affairs reporter at *The Daily Standard*. Dylan, it was well known, was the main reservoir for Debeers' leaks, and he occasionally attended the benchers' public meetings, mostly for the food and gossip, and to put everybody straight on whatever was under discussion. "The umbrella was rigged up like a little gun, see?"

"Gives a whole new meaning to the word *bumbershoot*, anyway," Fitz-Niblick said, chortling at his own joke.

This seems to have been hilarious to the assembled crowd, too, or at least they pretended so, blinking and bowing at their leader — who, after all, dictated the benchers' agenda and appointed all committee chairpersons. Faddaster, however, did not join in the general toadying, not because he was above it, but because, as usual, he was distracted by his own brilliance. "And the guy was a Bulgarian journalist, in fact," he went on. "Not Hungarian." Probably no one understood this bit of pedantry, for at the same moment Faddaster was sinking his incisors into a salmon salad sandwich triangle, courtesy of the membership's annual fees, no doubt much to the indignation of absent bencher Jeremiah Debeers.

"What's that?" Nobb said.

Faddaster took a swig from a can of Diet Pepsi. He affected an addiction to the cola as part of his hilariously futile ruse to make the world believe he was not a raging alcoholic. "He was Bulgarian." He swallowed and belched. "A Bulgarian broadcaster."

"Whatever," Eleanor Rorschach-Bulwark said, turning away and wiping her mouth with the Society's monogrammed linen.

"Anyway, the umbrella acted as this sort of rifle," Faddaster continued, then looked up at the beamed ceiling and old wooden clock hanging chandelier-style above them in the grand hall. "Or syringe, I suppose. It shot a little bullet with the poison in it, into this fellow's, this Bulgarian's, leg. A little pellet, sort of like a tiny whiffle ball, I've seen the photo, filled with some really lethal poison."

"Be the first time the old Splinter had any balls, eh?" Nobb whispered to Fitz-Niblick, who laughed out loud.

"Ricin," Faddaster was saying, eating again, a cocktail-portion quiche, this time, and nobody bothered to try to understand him. "That stuff the Algerian terrorists were manufacturing in London a couple of years ago. Ricin."

The others had begun moving away as Faddaster said, "Manufactured from the common castor bean, you know. It's quite simple to make, in fact. Chemically, I mean. Easy as pie."

I find the perfect fit on the bottom shelf a couple of yards behind the photocopier. I slip unobtrusive and as statuesque as the cat-goddess Set into the gap between *Irish Law Recorder, The* and *Louisiana Law Review, The*, where I supervise while the paramedics set up their stretcher at the front of the Journals Room.

"Could be a garden-variety infarc," one of them says, kneeling beside the corpse, "although the body's more contorted than you'd expect. Could be he had a lot of acute pain, writhed around or whatever."

"You mean from a heart attack, like?" a constable who arrived on the 9-1-1 call says, then bites into an apple, showering the vicinity with fruit juice.

The paramedic blinks. "Yeah. I mean, there's nothing else really obvious."

"Looks like something black on his hand there," the constable says, chewing. "Is that anything?"

"It's anything, yeah. Definitely recent. Palm's burned. Comes off on my finger, see? Got his wrist, too. Bruises here as well, see?" The paramedic looks up from the body and says: "I mean, it's up to you, constable, but I think you might want to get your scene investigation guys out. I mean, I don't know, but maybe you want to call in Homicide or whatever it is you do."

"You been watching to much TV, bud." The constable chews on his apple, smiling vaguely, or maybe sarcastically. Then he gestures with his snack and says through the mush, "I can call for a coroner's warrant, though, you know, get some forensics down here, if there's anything unusual."

"Well, that's the thing. I can't say there is anything unusual. Maybe it's nothing. Thing is, I just don't know."

"Why? What else you got?"

"Well, see, his hand was sort of jammed in behind the machine, like he was clutching at the back of it or something when he died. When I pulled it out, well, it had this black on it. Like I say, maybe it's something, maybe it's nothing. But I don't think I should move him just yet."

"Got his clothing, too, looks like," the homicide detective, a female Has-being, says when she arrives, to find the field pathologist examining the Splinter's corpse. "The cuff and part of the sleeve there, they're blackened."

"Could be he just hurt himself on the machine here," the pathologist says. Without looking up from the body, he pulls the coroner's warrant from his shirt pocket and hands it up to the detective. "Burned himself, maybe, either in bracing himself, or while he was trying to photocopy something, or his hand fell behind it or underneath where it was hot from use. Maybe it had been running a lot, or was in disrepair. I mean, I don't think it tells us much."

"Could it be just toner?"

"Could be. We'll have to look into it. Could be he was lying on the machine for a bit, sick or dead, before he went down to the floor. Then again, maybe there was just something really mind-blowing in that book there, and he just keeled over from the shock of it. Ka-blooey." He glances up, smiling over the bencher as was, now just another workaday stiff.

"You're just trying to impress me again with that fancy medical terminology stuff, right?" the detective says, a little flirtatiously. Then, abruptly, she is all business again, calling harshly to somebody else, presumably a forensic evidence techie: "You dust the top of the photocopier yet, Nick?" Just as they say that victims suffer a second violation in the witness box, the alternately grim and bantering commotion seem to kill Jeremiah Debeers a second time.

Receiving an affirmative answer, and the reassurance that the book on the photocopier's glass has been dusted and photographed so that it is ready for bagging and labelling, the detective takes a closer look. I had already noted that the so-called book is some sort of ledger, bound in old and tattered black cloth which is coming away at the binding so that its cardboard guts show through. "Wolf Blass Red Label Cab. S.," the detective reads, "2001."

The pathologist smacks his lips as he squints at Jerry Debeers' right hand and arm. "Nice little unassuming Aussie wine. Cabernet Sauvignon. Good value. Even police doctors with usurious mortgages can afford it."

"Somebody must agree with you," the detective answers. "It says there's five cases of it in inventory."

"I think you'll find that there *were* five cases. Have a look in the columns to the right. Some of it's been sampled."

"Some kind of accounting ledger, is it, you think?"

"Cellar log. You know, to keep track of the inventory of wine."

"From where, I wonder." Flipping through the log, the detective whistles. "Holy moly, listen to this. Boo . . . sahjur . . ."

"Beauséjour-Duffau."

"Bowsayjurs-Doofoe 1961, half-case, value as of 2000, four thousand and five hundred dollars. And one bottle, I guess — 1985 Pee . . . Peetrus . . ."

"Pétrus."

"Paytroos." The detective laughs. "Sounds much tastier that way. Eight hundred and twenty-five dollars. Definitely for police chiefs only, without mortgages."

"This is the Law Society, kiddo," the pathologist says, glancing up once more from his work. "Money no object."

"Apparently it's the log from the benchers' wine cellar," the constable says, coming over for a look himself. "So says one of them that was friendly with the victim." He consults his notes. "Probert. Josey Probert. She was in earlier, after one of the librarians called her. She worked with the guy, apparently, and she's offered to go over with us to his mother's house, to break the news to her."

"Yeah, okay," the detective says. "While you're driving over there, see if this . . . Probert is it? See if she can shed any light on what he might have been doing with that log."

"Assuming he was doing anything with it."

The detective mocks the constable's pedantry. "Yes, yes, *assuming. . . .*"

"Well, it could have been there before he arrived, you know. And there's nothing — no copies of anything — in the collating bin on the machine there."

"Yeah, okay, true enough. We should have some prints back by tomorrow or so if they can get any off it. The log, I mean. That should tell us something. Whether he handled it or whatever."

The constable drops a quarter in the machine. "Still might have been there before he came in," he mutters. "Somebody else could have left it there." The machine eats his money but makes no other response. He pushes a button here, a button there, bangs on the coin return. Dead. Dead. Dead.

When they have gone, the constable's quarter suddenly clatters into the return, attracting my renewed attention. I paw at the return, knocking the quarter to the floor. Quickly losing interest in such kitten's play, I have another nosey around the *locus in quo*. Sniffing charcoal though poor Debeers has been removed to the morgue, I push my front half under the photocopier, feeling my way in the dark with my whiskers. Sure enough, the machine's under-carriage is blackened, as is the floor underneath. I back out and squeeze behind the thing, which is some impressive trick even for Your Lithe Interlocutor, as the machine stands out from the wall just the width of its electrical plug. Though comatose, it is still plugged in. So why is it as unresponsive as a dozing judge? Has it suffered a matching heart attack in sympathy with poor old Jerry Debeers? Detecting a more familiar pong, masked though it is by the strong scent of burnt metal and rubber, I'd guess, and linoleum and who knows what, I nose my way up the plug, *left right, north south*. At its base, and wrapped up the cord for another six inches, maybe, I find a crinkled sheet of metal. Foil, it is. Aluminum foil. *Right left west east.* Charred as though it has been thrown in the fire to roast corn or a potato, and a little aromatic of cooked cheese, perhaps. Poor old Splinter Debeers. *Foil, foiled, despoiled.* When the photocopier repairman arrives later that day, my discovery becomes public knowledge.

And of course the police hurriedly reconvene in the Journals Room, re-sealing it and looking grimly embarrassed over what they have missed. Once the repairman had unwrapped the blackened foil around the photocopier's cord, he found that someone had carefully shaven the insulation on the electrical wires within and had removed the gauze packing around them, then covered the stripped cord with the foil. There was no splicing or anything like that, just the exposed top surface of the wiring, with the foil wrapped around it all. And the ground wire had been cut clean through, rendering it useless.

"What in the heck's the point of that?" the lady plainclothes, Detective Sergeant Donovan, she seems to be called, asks the repairman. He has pulled the machine out from the wall again and turned it sideways, so its back end is fully exposed. Though the windows are sealed shut, we can hear Ernie the Voice of Doom starting up again outside with his megaphone and Biblical admonishments:

And we read in Jeremiah, chapter two-a, verse twelve-a: "Be astonished, O ye heavens, at this, and be horribly afraid, be ye very desolate, saith the Lord-a."

"Well," the photocopy man answers, from a repairman's squat as he waggles the plug in his hand, "if you stripped all the wiring, they'd touch, see, the various wires would, see, and short out."

"But you just told us the whole machine shorted out anyways," Sergeant Donovan says. "The internal fuses blew, you said."

"I know. That's what I mean. I don't see how it would've shorted out just from this. The insulation is three-quarters intact, and nothing's touching anything else."

"So how would it have shorted out then?"

"Well, if it was plugged in and something or somebody squeezed the foil against it, you know, touched it, it would complete the circuit."

A wonderful and horrible thing is committed in the land-a!

"If the foil was wrapped lightly around it, like, before it was touched, or the power was shut off until that point. And then, if you squeezed the wires while the juice was back on, they would probably short out. The aluminum's all black, here, see, at the points of contact, as though somebody took hold of the foil?"

"Why would anybody do something stupid like that?" the sergeant asks.

Be astonished, O ye heavens-a, at this, and be horribly afraid-a!

"The thing is," Elise Throckmorton, Research Librarian, says, "when it's pushed against the wall the way it's supposed to be, reaching in there, you wouldn't see the foil. If you see what I mean."

As I always say, if you don't know the answer, ask a librarian.

CHAPTER 3

Damage Control

Progress is slow on "Environmentalist Protesters and the *Public Lands Act*." In fact, we are still on page nine, and our calendar indicates that the paper was due yesterday. Well, to be fair, there was *Streudel Investments v. 090567132 Ontario Ltd.*, deliberations and writing out our decision, seventy-eight single-spaced pages plus scores of hours squandered on a shareholder dispute among six members of the same family who had named their holding company after the youngest daughter's gerbil, which had died shortly thereafter. Fifteen years later, when the daughter and her two brothers grew up, the bad gerbil-omen played itself out in a bitter family feud, over whose shares could vote, who had effective corporate control, and especially why Dad (whom, sighing, we compared more than once to Job) finally got thoroughly disgusted and stopped declaring dividends in favour of his squabbling off-spring and spouse. And then there were two dozen other motions to hear, besides, as well as argument in a dispute about re-opening a separation agreement twenty years after the parties divorced (the husband coincidentally having become stinking rich on liquidating his stock options in a computer software business), and a three-day appeal of a libel judgment that pitted the *Daily Standard* against a former dictator, and now purported refugee of an obscure, fly-blown African nation latterly under French control. And then we were on a panel called "The View from the Bench," advising barristers on the methods of posturing and pandering which are most likely to succeed during uncivil litigation, as it has become. (We pined for the old days, when one dressed for court as for church and the judges were all My Lord: "You knew where you were then," we sighed before the Civil Litigation Section of the Bar Association. I had wandered in for this bit, given that it was in the Barrister's Lounge, just through the tunnel to the little tower between the Hall and the bigger courthouse at 361 University, the one you always see on television, where they hold the lurid murder and rape trials. "Public access to justice is very much to be encouraged," we admitted, "but preferably in a suit and tie, subsequent to a thorough shower and shave. A lawsuit is not the Jerry Springer Show.") And then there are those dirty, scruffy, decidedly uncivil squirrels.

The apricots have grown, and some even show a little brown on their shanks, if an apricot can be said to ripen in such an felixomorphic fashion. His Lordship* has instructed the gardeners to discourage the squirrels with various noxious dusts, powders and snow-fencing, and actively to shoo them away with threats and menaces whenever possible. The judge's clerk has been enlisted in the cause, the spectral, and not a little scare-crowish, Mr. Leland

---

*Note to file: I, too, am a traditionalist, of course, and if I had thumbs, I'd double-thumb down the Chief Justice's practice direction that these days all judges of the higher courts are to be known as "Your Honour" and "Justice" without reference to their sex. Sex, after all, is life itself.

Gaunt — well-called, given that he is thin to the point of translucence, seldom sees the sunlight, and, when he isn't haunting the library and squinting at the *Dominion Law Reports* through his beer-bottle spectacles, has a tendency to creep in and out of His Lordship's chambers on little cat feet, spreading about his little gifts of prey from his diurnal adventures — computer diskettes crammed byteless with his obscure researches; cryptic memoranda of law, single-spaced, crumpled, torn at their edges; law books clownishly festooned with cryptic notes on sticky papers of various colours — yellow for "supports appellant's argument," pink for "supports respondent's argument," purple for "equivocal or ambiguous — could go either way," and so on. But despite this determined campaign, His Lordship's War on Squirrelly Terrorism remains fruitless, pun shamelessly intended. Said rodents continue to devour the apricot kernels and discard the ruined fruit for the gardeners to compost. And such is His Lordship's rage and frustration today that he throws himself against the sashed window, forcing it open by furiously splintering away a half-century, at least, of caulk, plaster, and paint, hollering and waving his hands like a madman at the pillaging rodents below. This attracts the attention of passersby, including several robed barristers who wave back and shout, "Good morning, Your Honour" and such. The squirrels remain oblivious. They are preoccupied, after all, with stripping the apricot trees.

As I watch from His Lordship's desk, he runs to a corner of his chambers and retrieves his running shoes from his gym bag under the coat tree. Then, one at a time, he throws the sneakers out the window, bellowing inarticulately. One shoe hits the unfortunate Mr. Gaunt, who is on his way back from the law library at the University of Toronto and no doubt wonders what idiocy he has committed this time — some error, probably, that will blot his entire career at the bar before it has begun. A couple of pigeons briefly flap themselves a few inches off the ground, and a little black squirrel with a truly pitiable case of the mange jumps straight up in the air, but that's probably because poor Gaunt's cry of startled pain shoots across the forecourt like an antiballistic missile. A couple of the other squirrels pause briefly before resuming their apricot-kernel breakfast.

When Jerry Debeers ran for bencher, he wrote a candidate profile of himself for the voters' guide the Law Society mails to its lawyer-members. Elise Throckmorton consults a copy as Sergeant Donovan questions her at her cubicle just north of the Duck Blind. "You can keep this, if you want," Elise says. "We've got plenty. And they're irrelevant space-wasters at this point."

"Thank you, I will. As for these committees it says he was on, they were committees here at the Law Society? 'Discipline Committee,' what's that?"

"It's like a panel of judges, or a jury. They hear discipline proceedings against lawyers — you know, lawyers accused of screwing up or whatever."

"Or screwing around," the sergeant says, leafing through the guide. Elise does not respond. "'Admissions Committee. Chair, Hospitality Committee and Vice-chair, Sub-committee on Strategic Use of Convocation Hall.' What would that be about?"

"You'll have to ask the treasurer, Mr. Fitz-Niblick. All I know is that they were looking at whether they should privatize the food service and the hall rental. You know, privatize Convocation Hall, which becomes the Barrister's Dining Room at lunchtime. They were debating whether they should continue to run it themselves or contract it out. I know it was very controversial, and Mr. Debeers wrote an article in the *Law Society Gazette* against privatizing it. He was quite passionate about it, I seem to recall — especially about the need not to put it into the hands of a few profiteers, moneychangers, he called them. He thought it was another way the profession was losing self-control and self-determination. Selling out to big business and all that, I suppose. But that's about all I can tell you about it."

"That's fine. We'll talk to Mr. Fitz-Niblick, then."

I wander over for a gander at Jerry's profile from behind the detective's shoulder. Conveniently (and as planned), she thinks I am there for base epicurean motives, *id est*, that I merely want stroking. *Ronronner ronronner ronronner.* But as far as a cat's concerned, *everything* is premeditated.

> **For** [Debeers' profile reads,]: Mandatory refresher course in Professional Ethics.
>
> **Against:** Bencher remuneration. Last year's bylaw authorizing benchers to draw an "honorarium" of $25,000 annually should be repealed. Serving the profession is a rare honour in itself, as well as a duty that should be its own reward. Election as a bencher already carries material rewards, such as an enhanced professional profile and the opportunity for high-level networking.
>
> ["Seems a curious view," I remember Justice Mariner

remarking at election time, "for a guy with a faltering law practice. You'd think he'd want to get paid."]

For: A greater voice for the small practitioner.

Against: Dominance of law society affairs by the big Bay Street firms.

For: Greater regulation of bencher spending on high-profile programs and functions. This would make possible a *fee reduction for all members,* which is central to my platform.

Against: Greater Law Society regulation of members' affairs. We are seriously over-regulated and over-taxed by high dues and errors-and-omissions insurance premiums.

For: Abolition of Sunday meetings of the Society committees. The Lord's Day should be returned to the Lord and our family life.

Against: Privatization of Convocation Hall and the related food and hospitality services.

Hobbies, extracurricular activities: "Lawyers Feed the Hungry" program; model trains; walking; reading; early music, esp. choral and sacred; playing guitar.

"They called him the Splinter, I hear," Sergeant Donovan remarks, still perusing the profile, and sneering a little, I would say. "He doesn't sound so wild and woolly to me."

"I don't know what they called him," Elise replies. "But he provoked a lot of discussion, that's for sure. I think he saw himself as David versus the Goliath of the big business firms. The Establishment lawyers. Then again, a lot of lawyers, especially in the smaller firms, or sole practitioners, they liked him a lot, you know. They supported him. They were his constituency."

"Makes sense." The sergeant nods and smiles, although her eyes look like clots of molten iron.

"And he always treated staff here with respect. We knew him quite well, in fact — me, Katrina, and Elizabeth, our head librarian. Face to face, well" — a single, reluctant tear escapes Elise Throckmorton's right eye — "yeah, he was a nice guy. Decent. A little uptight, maybe. But he really was a decent man."

What Elise Throckmorton does not tell the police is that her view of the legal profession in general remains rather more jaundiced, at least from her unique perspective in the Duck Blind. This becomes clear to me when Katrina Slovenskaya returns to the Great Library after two days of stress leave, plus the weekend.

"So what are you doing back here already?" Elise asks her, wild-eyed, glancing accusingly at Chief Librarian Elizabeth Bane, over tea and shortbread from the red plaid tin, a relic of some Christmas past. "You crazy or what?"

At the moment, the chief, who is a little older than Elise and decidedly more middle class in demeanour and dress, is inserting her incisors into a biscuit. Looking alarmed, Bane waves a hand before her mouth and chews much too rapidly to justify the calorie intake. Swallowing as much of the shortbread as she can in one go, she protests, "Thee wanted t' come back herthelf!"

"It's true," Katrina admits. "There was no point moping around home. I'd rather keep busy."

"See!" the chief librarian tries to say. "It wath her deethithon." She sips at her tea.

"Hey, but what about the lawyer you were helping at the time? The guy with the mortgage problem."

"You mean the guy I was with when we went into the Journals Room? The guy *you sent me down there with?*" Katrina can't help pulling a face at her colleague, although she doesn't quite manage to glare.

"Yeah. The Saudi Arabian mortgage guy. Hey, how was I to know?"

Katrina shakes her head and shrugs. "Disappeared."

"Isn't that just typical?" the chief says, having cleared her palate with milky tea.

"He did mention, though," Katrina looks at her hands, "that he knew Jerry vaguely. Seems he was in some trouble, this mortgage guy, I mean, with the discipline committee. Over some house deal that went sour. And Jerry was chairing the discipline committee or something."

It's Elise's turn to shake her head and swallow biscuit. "They fly in here, all out of breath, their robes in a major flap, and they want you to do three weeks' research for them in ten minutes."

"It goes without saying that their own participation is limited to standing grimly over you, melodramatically checking their wristwatches," Katrina agrees, nodding and munching away.

"Of course that doesn't stop them bragging to their client later, how their brilliant research won the day in court," Elizabeth adds.

True enough, this species of barrister is as common in our Great Library as pigeons at the bird feeder. "You know," Elise says, smiling dreamily, naughtily, "I sometimes fantasize about revenge."

"Don't we all?" the chief asks, rolling her eyes.

"No, seriously," Elise says, laughing, but with a steely glint in her eye. "I could write a murder mystery. *Murder at Osgoode Hall.*"

Katrina stops chewing and looks at her lap. Elise doesn't seem to notice.

"The heroine, of course, is a research librarian."

"Do tell," says the chief.

"It opens in the Reference Room, see. A barrister not unlike Katrina's . . ." Elise arches her eyebrows, holding up her hands. "I mean *our* mortgage guy, he comes flying in, sweating like a Pony Express horse. The tie's flying, the oversized white shirt's pulled up from the waistband of the trousers. There're ringlets of sweat around the armpits."

The librarians giggle.

Ah, yes, where have we seen that one?

"Let's see, now, where've I seen that before?" the chief asks, dunking her shortbread.

"He's panting and wheezing from carrying this briefcase that looks like King Kong's picnic hamper. And he runs up to our hero, Jane Dewey-Decimal, Reference Librarian, and he wheezes, 'Real estate.'"

The chief laughs, nearly choking on her biscuit, wagging her finger at Elise, whose eyes are half-closed as she tells her revenge fable. Katrina finally looks up from her lap and attempts a smile.

"Jane is amazing, of course."

"Natch," the chief says, chewing.

"She doesn't bat an eye. She's seen this a thousand times, at least. You can almost see her grit her teeth a little, maybe, but she smiles and gently asks the fidgeting, panting barrister exactly what aspect of real estate he has in mind."

"That would help," the chief puts in. Katrina nods a little sadly, her hands folded limply before her. It's all too familiar.

"The guy swallows hard and gives Jane a look like she must be lobotomized to be so stupid. Then he catches his breath and manages to gasp, 'Financing. Priorities. Loans.' Well, the librarian still doesn't flinch, of course."

"'Course not."

"If anything, her smile brightens. A light has come on in her eyes. She tells the lawyer she knows just the thing. It's downstairs. Would he like to follow her?"

I quietly growl. This seems a little close to the bone, no? More than a little cruel? Given recent events, isn't it a little premature for gallows humour? Katrina is examining her hands in her lap now, as though they are detached objets d'art.

"Of course this fantasy used to be better in the pre-renovation days."

I am told on reliable authority — well, by an old familiar of these parts, anyway, a stray tom called Baudelaire who's been around town and has the demonstrative evidence to prove it, insofar as he's missing one eye, suffers from glaucoma in the other, and the top halves of both his ears have been razored off in street melees — Baudelaire tells me that the librarians used to call the old downstairs, where they kept the circulating books, Death Valley. *Had all the ambience of an unlit underground parking garage in the warehouse district,* Baudelaire says. Such a muddle of narrow corridors and dead ends, so mysteriously arranged in the obscure and lonely finster that even the librarians couldn't find their way without a map and compass.

"Anyway, our heroine," Elise is saying, "leads the steaming real estate researcher downstairs to this lonely and isolated room full of shelving and old stacks of boxes where slasher-maniacs in hockey masks could hide for days. And of course the guy never returns. He just disappears." She throws her empty hands merrily in the air and smiles toothily at her colleagues. For the first time, I notice a defect in her ethereal beauty. One of her upper teeth, at the left side, is higher than the others, a useless little runt. "Nobody misses him for a couple of years, of course, and by that time the only clue left is a little blood and toupee hair on a blunt instrument."

The chief is riveted. She sits forward with her mouth open, a biscuit poised at her chin. "What blunt instrument?" she pants, opening her mouth still wider.

Elise claps her hands, springing the trap. "The 1963 edition of *Falconbridge on Mortgages*. What else?"

The chief hardly waits a beat to step on the joke. "And she gets away with it?"

"Well, duh! It's the perfect crime, isn't it?" Elise leans forward and speaks more softly. "Because only the librarians know about the blunt instrument. They keep it on the shelf as a silent monument to a great victory for their side. In the bowels of their library. It's their secret."

"A memento mori," the chief whispers from a far-away territory in her mind.

"As they well know, no other real estate lawyer will ever find it because those guys never do their own research!"

She and the chief laugh gaily. Katrina smiles vaguely at them, nods, then walks deliberately, slowly back to her desk.

෧ᘊᘊ෧

"Jesus," Nobb says, as he takes his usual seat next to Treasurer Fitz-Niblick.

"You can say that again," the treasurer says.

"Jesus," Nobb says, but not to be funny. He isn't listening to anything but his own stunned thoughts, his eyes blindly fixed on the oak bookcases across the room. Of course, he's also a little tiddly from the four glasses of Spanish plonk he imbibed with his lunch. "Jesus H. Christ."

"And you can forget anything I said about bumbershoots or the defence of provocation." The treasurer nods abruptly, his lips pursed. He will have enjoyed just one glass, but of a very fine Beaune burgundy, savoured.

"Electrocuted, they think," Nobb chunters on, his eyes still unblinking, unseeing. "Jesus. The guy was a bit of a pain, yeah, but I wouldn't have wished this on him. Poor son of a bitch."

"Apparently it could have been a heart attack." The treasurer taps at the side of his nose to indicate that this earth-shattering speculation is confidential. "The electrical shock itself might not have been enough to do it, is what I've just been told."

Nobb shushes him in any event as Josey Probert enters the meeting room. She is small and tightly wound, a not-unattractive woman in her mid forties, her mouse-brown hair cut short and elegantly styled, with just enough grey to give her a bit of the bencher's *gravitas*. Her face is artfully made up, but her eyes are red rimmed around the dark liner, and as she greets her colleagues she weeps silently, shaking her head and wafting expensive perfume. "I can't believe it," she says. "I just talked to him yesterday afternoon.

It's like a bad dream." She and Eleanor Rorschach-Bulwark hug.

"The police'll probably want to know that," says Bencher Abramowitz, a small, nondescript, mild-mannered fellow with a general law practice of the same character. "That you talked to him yesterday, I mean."

"I don't see why," Probert answers, glaring.

"Can I have everyone's attention please, ladies and gentlemen?" Treasurer Fitz-Niblick surveys the room in a commanding fashion. "Thank you. I now call this extraordinary session of Convocation to order. Thank you."

Your Honorary Feline Bencher settles in against the sideboard, having hustled here as soon as I caught wind of the special confab. No cream, milk, or chocky biscuit has yet been spilt, but it's early days. "As many of you will know, I am sure," Treasurer Fitz-Niblick begins, "the Law Society has suffered a great tragedy today. It is my sad duty to confirm that our friend and colleague, Jerry Debeers, has passed away."

"But is it true that he died in the toilets, Sammy, in the basement, in the education wing?" I recognize the questioner, a large, literal-minded man from the northeast region, but I don't know his name.

"The toilets?" Nobb is aghast, wishing he'd finished the bottle.

"The Bar Admission Course toilets, I heard," the man says. "In the basement."

"I thought it was in the Great Library," Nobb says, and looks fearfully from face to face around the table, his mouth open. "On the first floor."

The treasurer holds up his hand. "We can't get into a lot of detail just now," he says, "because it's still being looked into. But yes, it was in the library. And we will keep you posted as we learn more. The immediate problems before us are two, however, and that's why I called this special meeting. First, we have to decide how we want to present this business publicly. There are some complicated details involved, and the police don't want them getting out, until they investigate more thoroughly."

"Complicated how?" Josey Probert asks. She sounds angry, but it might just be her grief, of course.

"As I say," the treasurer replies, "we can't get into that just now. The police are playing their cards close to their chests for the time being. Josey, as Jerry's good friend, do you think you could compose some sort of press release, something appropriately dignified?"

"Yes, of course."

"Maybe Roman can help you on that."

"My pleasure," Nobb says, seeming to find a foothold, if a rocky one. He nods vaguely at Probert, his eyes still not quite focussed.

"I don't imagine we need to vote on that, do we?" Treasurer Fitz-Niblick asks. Several of the benchers shake their heads. "Good. It's arranged, then. And I'd suggest we have something ready to go in the next couple of hours, if you don't mind. Damage control, you know. Then I'll pass it along to the society's communications people to release. I'll tell them that it's politically sensitive and all that, and we don't want it changed."

"Has somebody arranged for flowers and a card to the mother?" Probert asks.

"Oh, right," Fitz-Niblick says, "Can someone look after that?

"Never mind," Probert volunteers. "I'll do it. I've met her on a couple of occasions."

"Josey, I assume you might also want to help with the winding up of his law practice," Abramowitz says.

"What there is of it," Nobb can't resist muttering to no one in particular, with an arch look suddenly animating his ramshackle face. Then he puts his hand judo-chop style next to his mouth and whispers lubriciously to those windward of Abramowitz, "Nothing there to skim off for yourself, Mr. Moneychanger, sir."

The impish, usually laconic, Bencher McKeen has overheard him. "Only the sour cream," he replies, winking.

"I can help, too, if need be," Abramowitz offers. "I'm just down the street from you folks." Probert, it seems, shared office space with the deceased. McKeen rolls his eyes at Nobb, who smirks back, although he still looks quite seasick.

"That's okay, Solly." The treasurer shakes his head. "Roman and I are already looking after it. It's all taken care of."

Maybe it's my imagination, or my non-Has-being perception, but this seems to be news to Nobb. Mind you, just about everything seems to be news to Nobb. It's not his fault, of course. Someone has been filtering reality for him from birth. Insulation is a fact of his life. "The help" has always been there, whether in the form of a nanny, Daddy, the Club, his artist-wife Marilyn, or Nobb's legal secretaries, who no doubt have served him incidentally as everything from second wives to I wouldn't like to say. Yes, it would be a serious mistake to underestimate him: thirty-eight years at the bar have made him worldly enough that he does not employ bimbos, whores, or fools. He knows he can't afford them. Still, wealth creates its own cocoon.

Josey Probert, meanwhile, does not hide her surprise that Debeers' practice is already seen to. Nor does she mask her displeasure. Noticing this, Eleanor Rorschach-Bulwark hisses to her, "But the flowers and card are women's work, I guess."

Probert frowns, then responds to Rorschach-Bulwark without looking at her, shaking her head: "The man's hardly cold, for God's sake."

"But what does he mean," Bulwark asks, "'damage control'?"

Probert does not get time to reply. "The second consideration," Treasurer Fitz-Niblick is saying the while, "is an interim appointment to fill his position. For one thing, he had a couple of discipline matters he was supposed to be sitting on during the next few weeks."

"A real estate deal gone down the Swanee," Nobb whispers to McKeen. "That was one of them."

I lose interest and doze. When a hospitality server wheels in the cart with coffee and pastries, leaving the door ajar, I make good my escape, toward the Barrister's Dining Room, alias Convocation Hall and its lunchtime kitchen, a sure and better thing.

Having somehow caught wind of the funereal happenings, Dylan Faddaster, the *Daily Standard* hack, is seated at one of the dining tables, drinking tea and waiting on Fitz-Niblick or whoever else he can buttonhole once the extraordinary convocation breaks up. Meanwhile, he regales Jean-Pierre, the law society's notoriously ferocious maître-d', with memories of the various joke stratagems proposed for doing away with the Splinter. Faddaster has just explained to the annoyed and mostly inattentive Belgian émigré, who periodically and fruitlessly tries to signal with his lurching body that he is meant to be setting up for lunch, how the Israeli Mossad kill their adversaries by planting bombs in cell-phones, which they then explode by remote control when the target answers. Faddaster then switches enthusiastically to the chatter at a recent reception held in Convocation Hall itself to celebrate Treasurer Fitz-Niblick's new book, *Wealth Management and the Law of Estates*.

I had attended the event myself, or wandered through it, anyway. The whole "put the hit on Jerry" joke was a commonplace by then and had reached the level of farce, with Faddaster constantly goading it to new lows. Once it was clear that Debeers was not present at the party (Faddaster explains to the ensnared Jean-Pierre, who shifts from foot to foot and frowns as though he has a serious bowel disorder), the conversation turned once again to colourful ways of eliminating him.

"'Maybe you could do the opposite of what the CIA tried to do to Castro,' I was telling some of the guests." I had witnessed this myself, and he wasn't exaggerating — or, anyway, he was giving the impatient maître-d' a faithful account. Faddaster had joined a group assembled near the drinks table, and as he talked he spat cocktail peanuts hither and yon at the benchers, their spouses, and representatives of Fitz-Niblick's publishers. He towered over the crowd, fat, bearded, and bespectacled, a ramshackle man, haggard in the way of newspaper people of the nineteen-forties, his face dishevelled with disorganized thought and alcoholism. He shared with Debeers a taste for the outrageous, or, rather, for the attention it brought him, although from the polar opposite view, the Devil's advocate view, you might say, as against Debeers' self-righteous piety. "Remember — how they tried to make Castro's beard fall off? Or they planned to make his beard fall off. Put explosives in his cigars or something, like in a cartoon. The CIA."

"As you might have noticed, Dylan, Jerry is clean-shaven," one of the party-goers had remarked.

"That's what I mean, see. You could do the opposite, give him a beard, make him grow such a heavy beard, put something in his food or whatever, steroids, I guess, so he always has five o'clock shadow, like Yasser Arafat. People'd come to see him as the sneaky little terrorist he is. Psychologically, it'd freak him right out, too. He'd think it was a judgment of God. And I'm pretty sure, with steroids, he'd eventually croak of liver failure. Eventually. Game over."

"One more little hitch there, Dylan, old man," came the reply. "Larry doesn't smoke."

"Doesn't smoke," someone else said, "drink, eat red meat . . ."

"All right, then. What about the old icicle to the brainpan manoeuvre? Quicker and surer, doesn't have to ingest anything, and the weapon melts without a trace. The perfect crime. That's how they got rid of Trotsky."

"That was an ice-*pick*, Dylan," someone pointed out.

"Hey, same diff. And Debeers is your sort of local Trotskyite, right?, fundamentalist communalist or whatever. Dogmatist. And this is Canada, so you can use a melting weapon. No prints, either. Hey-o, the perfect crime."

"Much too messy. Blood. Water damage. The members would have to foot the cleaning bill, which would drive the Splinter crazy, even in the afterlife. And we'd never hear the end of it from his comrade, Josey Probert."

"It's quite a clean kill, actually," Faddaster replied in all seriousness.

"But the blood . . ."

"None, if you do it right." Faddaster shook his head, shotgunning more peanut bits so that the scrum took another step back from him. "Sharpen the sucker up and one determined push under the base of the skull, like this," he demonstrated on the publisher's cranium, "or through the ear, and Bob's your uncle."

"Well, Faddy, we'd need a real Stalinist for a job like that," Nobb said. "Someone with the necessary commitment, the congenital *sang froid*, someone who could protect his sources." The scrum stared significantly at the journalist, fully enjoying the irony.

"I appreciate the compliment, folks, but you know very well that I can't be trusted," Faddaster said, sincerely, chastened only a little.

"And do you never stop eating?" Rorschach-Bulwark asked him, no doubt brushing peanut from her blouse.

"Have some." Chewing, he proffered a handful of the Virginia peanuts, in the skin.

"Thank you, no." The lady pulled a face at his greasy, ink-stained hand.

"Mr. Peters?" The journalist wiped his opposite salty hand on his trousers.

"But they're rancid!" Peters, principal of Devillers Publishing, spat legumes on the floor of the Great Hall.

"To all these refined Queen's Counsel tastes here, perhaps. Mother's milk to me."

"Yes," said Nobb. "You're bilious, you are."

"But that's it!" Faddaster spewed a new nut-volley. "It's perfect. That's it! *Aspergillus flavus. The Human Factor.* Bile. I think we've got it. Exactly what you're looking for."

"By George, he's got it! He's really got it!" Fitz-Niblick, the man of the hour, chimed in, waltzing giddily over with his glass of

1997 Corton, courtesy of the Benchers' wine cellar, and doing a passable Rex Harrison. "Asparagus afflatus."

The journalist sang, spitting peanut: "The rain in Spain stays mainly on the asparagus patch."

"But he's very abstemious, is our Splinter," Nobb cautioned. "They're not joking about that."

"I'm well aware of that, Mr. Nobb," Faddaster said.

"Doesn't share your fondness for food and drink, particularly not on the members' tab, as he calls it."

"So he tells me," Fitz-Niblick admitted, raising his fine wine to his audience of pursed lips, "and tells me. But go on, then," Fitz-Niblick said, as we pricked up our ears. "Tell us all about it, then, this asparagus flavus. I know you will, anyway, Faddy."

"Simple," Faddaster said. "It's how they get rid of a suspected double agent, I think it is, in *The Human Factor*, by Graham Greene. The double agent is a borderline alcoholic, see, a risk to national security, and he knows that they, the other agents, he knows they might be onto him. So they decide to get rid of him with this peanut toxin. When peanuts go off, they produce this extremely toxic mould, see. It can kill you inside a week."

"*Aspergillus flavus*, I presume," said Fitz-Niblick, saluting the assemblage with his Corton once more, then sipping at it.

"It's an aflatoxin. It kills the liver," Faddaster explained, as the others began drifting away. "Looks like cirrhosis. Less than a milligram of the stuff will do it."

But by then, having heard it all before, I had moved on to my target destination.

⌒◌⌒

Lunch was at its peak of hurly-burly when I moseyed back out of the kitchen a little later and began crossing the packed dining hall toward my lair in the Great Library. Until the benchers had elected Fitz-Niblick as Law Society treasurer, the dining room and related catering services had almost always run at a loss, with only the occasional barrister and his clients coming in for a quick bite between the morning and afternoon court sessions. It was an expensive, and exclusive, luxury. The dining room, with its burnished oak panelling, opera theatre balconies, and cathedral-style vaulting truss ceiling, was constructed in the early eighteen-eighties. It originally functioned as an examination and assembly room: hence its more formal moniker, Convocation Hall. Three stories beneath its oak floor lies that well-stocked wine cellar at the benchers' disposal. The weighty Victorian splendour, made all the more grave by massive, gilt-framed portraits of the Chief Justices of Upper Canada, was brightened during the nineteen-eighties by the addition of ten stained-glass windows (again, in the cathedral manner), depicting, says the society's tourist brochure, "various aspects of Canadian legal heritage."

Working with (or, as the treasurer often saw it, against) Jerry Debeers as co-chair of the Hospitality Committee, and on the philosophy of spending money to make money, Fitz-Niblick had put the grand facility even deeper in the red. First, he hired Jamie Weissbrot, one of the young Turk breed of head chefs so trendy these days, away from the chi-chi L'Attitude, on Yonge Street in mid-town, along with L'Attitude's redoubtable Jean-Pierre to run the actual dining room. Then, without consulting the membership, which Fitz-Niblick predicted accurately would oppose him, the treasurer threw the doors wide open to the public, bringing in a $3,500-a-day PR firm to get the word out. Weissbrot attracted the food reviewers, including Faddaster, who wrote memorably that "the French fries in my pita stir-fry reminded me of that Scottish national dish, the chip butty, alias, the French fry sandwich. But what the hey, Robbie Burns ate those for breakfast and it didn't stop him from becoming Poet Laureate. And the crème caramel was to die for, particularly if you've got stage-two diabetes like yours truly."

The genuine food critics had fewer reservations, which everyone else suddenly needed, even if they were ageing barristers like Roman Nobb, Queen's Counsel, and Justice Ted Mariner, who had been wandering into the dining room at will for twenty-five years. Fitz-Niblick had his secretary post the critics' gushing reviews in the Law Society lobby and, suddenly, if you could find twenty minutes to grab a sandwich and bone up for afternoon court, you had to go across the street for your nosh. The erstwhile Barrister's Dining Room was booked solid with self-styled consultants and committee members of the ballet, symphony, and all the most fashionable charitable foundations (including Nobb's wife, Marilyn, a metal sculptor and chair of the regional Fine Arts Alliance), and other ladies who lunched. But it was still, or rather more deeply, shamelessly, in the red, a mistress of insatiable demands.

Seeing that Faddaster is still present, and lunching now with Josey Probert, I amble over for a *pro forma* beg, just so that I can turn my nose up at whatever they might deign to offer. It is, after all, part of my job description as resident Questing Cat. Truth to tell, I couldn't eat another morsel, not even if it were fresh popinjay tartare served up on Law Society bone china and placed under my nose on the venerable room's oak floor. The sous-chef has feted me from the Society's latest wheel of Grand Padano parmesan (40 bucks a pound, but, as he says, "it's the lawyers' money, not mine") grated onto some of today's warm Alfredo sauce, which I have awarded two vestigial thumbs up. Faddaster sucks at skeins of fettuccine dripping that concoction all over his white shirt front, navy trousers, and the linen tablecloth, as his luncheon companion, Bencher Probert, tries not to notice. I, however, enjoy the show for some moments, until Faddaster suddenly sucks his breath in and chokes on a knot of pasta, doubling over and spluttering away. He sucks air again, rises up in his chair, and coughs alfredo all over both the table and poor Josey. Then a look of shock freezes his red and aerated face as though he's at Alice Fazooli's trattoria and he's just taken a round from a .45 to his breadbasket. It must feel something like that, anyway, for after he at last gets his wind and hoovers back some water from his glass, he sets his fork down and hacks out, "Jesus *hack*. There must be something wrong with this fucking pasta *hack*. I've suddenly *hack hack* got a fucking bellyache like *hack* you wouldn't fucking *hack hack* believe *hack*. Out of nowhere, I mean *hack*. Like *hack*, it's just fucking weird. *Hack*."

Happily for Josey, she is having only a salad and mineral water, albeit now seasoned lightly with Alfredo sauce. "Are you going to be all right, Dylan?" she asks, her eyes struggling against their thick coatings of liner and shadow to flutter in alarm as Faddaster gulps away at his water, then at Probert's Perrier, then at a half-empty cup of cold coffee from the next table, just vacated but as a new group of diners arrives there, goggle-eyed and nervous for their safety. Standing, or crouching, really, Faddaster knocks his empty glass to the floor while reaching for his wallet. He flips thirty dollars onto the table. "You'll have to excuse me," he says, coughing and spluttering so violently that the room has gone quiet to watch him. "I've got to go be very sick, I'm afraid, preferably very nearby." He takes a few steps toward the Gents at the library side of the dining hall, then limps briefly to the table again and grabs back the twenty from his share of the bill, stuffing it into his sports jacket. "On second thought," he explains, panting and sweating, "I can get poisoned elsewhere in the neighbourhood, at half the cost."

At one third, by my arithmetic, but who's counting?

CHAPTER 4

In Wine, Truth!

A man who looks like Santa Claus in January . . . big and shop-worn, his eyes bloodshot and jaundiced over a Chassid's nicotine-stained beard sprawling across a short-sleeved shirt violent with vegetation, the tortured stems of which, on this mid-winter day, lead your eye irresistibly down from the crumpled hem to the wearer's crumpled chinos, to his heavy wool socks pulled up haphazard over the trouser bottoms, to his battered workboots . . . a man who looks like Santa Claus on an urgent holiday scowls down at His Lordship and me as we hunch over our morning crossword. And he says: "Madam, I'm Adam."

We are here to assist with the Thursday morning Out of the Cold breakfast in Osgoode's basement cafeteria, a hang-out for Bar Admission Course students, but otherwise a little-used facility. Having waited at table from six to eight a.m., serving pancakes, scrambled eggs, back bacon, fruit cup, and coffee to the assembled homeless or hungry, we are now enjoying a plate of same as the old tramp sits down, uninvited, across from us. I hike my eyebrows at him, who on top of everything else wheezes and stinks of Gauloise tobacco. "Morning," His Lordship responds cheerily, staring hard at his newspaper. Over his right arm the tramp carries a brittle and peeling hide coat, which grazes my scalp and smells like wet farm animals.

"Adam's hiccup," the bum wheezes, lighting the stub of what looks like a marijuana joint.

"Sorry?" Justice Mariner looks evenly up at him, trying to seem tolerant but busy, a man with important matters that need seeing to, although actually he is a man who has nothing at all in his diary today. We were supposed to hear that appeal by the ex-wife seeking to re-open her twenty-year-old separation agreement, but it was "put over" because of her suddenly wealthy husband's alleged influenza.

"Five down. 'Adam's hiccup.' Madam, I'm Adam." The tramp taps a nicotine-stained finger the size of a small sausage on His Lordship's newspaper.

"Oh, I see," the judge says, and, because politeness demands it and he is a polite if slightly pompous fellow, he pencils it in, *MADAMIMADAM*, the answer to the clue "Adam's hiccup." He smiles woodenly at his odoriferous helper and he thinks, smiling harder, *Damn*. I can see it in his eyes: *Damn*.

"Jocular linguist's term." The tramp squints through his own smog. "If that's not an oxymoron." You're not supposed to smoke in here, of course, but His Lordship thinks better of saying so. "Hard to imagine, isn't it, a jocular linguist? It means the first human utterance. Adam's hiccup. The first human utterance."

"I thought you meant your name was Adam," Justice Mariner says. *Adam Ziccov*. Personally, I had thought he'd said something about a stick-up, and I mew with relief, causing him to reach down and offer me a crumb of bacon from the table. I spit it on his torn boot, flapping away with my smouldering tongue, desperate to roust the Gauloises taste of his fingers and the sting of the bleach they use to clean the tables.

"Ernie Clochard," he says, thrusting a redolent orange paw at the judge. It is, in fact, Ernie the Evangelist, and I have wondered since if the surname isn't his *nom de guerre* — *clochard*, after the street philosophers of Paris, the deliberately homeless who eschew everything material for the life of the mind and soul. Sort of like the quintessential cat, I suppose, nature's *clochard*. "Jocular linguist," he says. "Philologist, really. Or, actually, these days, generalist. General researcher, I mean. Freelance, lately. Researcher, writer, consultant, public speaker. Have brains, will travel, as long as the subway, streetcar, or city bus goes there." Squinting, he draws on his home-made fag with impressive skill, considering that it is down to a scrap. "One is obliged to be flexible these days."

"One certainly is," the judge says, shaking the proffered paw, smiling a little grimly so that he seems to be grimacing in pain.

"Didn't get your moniker," Ernie says. Having only just finished his cigarette, he breathes sonorously as he rolls another on a little plastic machine he pulls from his vest. He drops his chin to his chest, the better to see his work, and so must glance at the judge by hiking up his wild eyebrows, showing eyesockets striated with blood. Meanwhile, the cigarette machine's wondrous simplicity fascinates me. It's nothing more complex than a blue rubber dam on a pair of rollers which spit out what I had earlier taken to be a reefer.

"Ted," the ancient Mariner replies. "Ted." His tongue sticks on the final d.

"You a lawyer, then, Ted?" A pungent, not unmarijuana-like

cloud hangs around us, daring anyone to complain.

To be fair, what Ted is is not obvious. We are in mufti today, this unexpected holiday, this day of soup kitchen charity — a plaid lumberjack shirt, blue jeans, and hiking boots. His Lordship thinks about Ernie's question for a moment and then risks honesty, more or less: "Yes, Ernie, for my sins."

"Sins, Ted. Don't talk to me of sins. That's all part of my day job, you see, and I'm off duty just now. Let me digest my breakfast first, please, sir, before we broach the subject of human sin. Please."

"Your day job, Ernie?"

"Freelance lecture circuit, Ted. Public, as I say, speaking. Lately, I've been considering the problem of whether we have turned our back on God, or whether He has, understandably, mind you, turned His back on us. You know, Nietszche, *Deus absconditus* and all that. God's disgust, or disinterest, perhaps. It troubles me, Ted, and I take the personal approach in my teaching. My method is, you might say, to wonder out loud. Sometimes to the consternation of the local constabulary, I must say."

"And what have you concluded, Ernie?"

"That I am a superstitious atheist, Ted. That I cannot forgive God for not existing." Ernie smiles, but his eyes remain solemn.

"I think I can understand that, Ernie." His Lordship nods and smiles wanly, considering the proposition. "That's very interesting. And, I would say, a not unreasonable conclusion."

"And that is why I am out on the people's lecture circuit, Ted, wondering aloud, trying to settle the thing in my own mind, seeking currency on it with the general public. Propheteering, as it were."

There is a long pause while Ernie smokes off the nub of his fag.

A few latecomers straggle in, freshly showered, neatly dressed, having just found their way to the Hall's east entrance, between New City Hall and the park where some of our "customers" have spent the night. Finally, Justice Mariner says to Ernie the Evangelist, "Actually, I thought Madam, I'm Adam was a palindrome. You know, same thing forward and back." The smile widens on his face and he seems to relax now, sincerely interested in Ernie Clochard's reply.

"Absolutely," Ernie says, as if it went without saying, and his own battered mug brightens. "Which is why your crossword designer thinks it's so clever. Never do crosswords, myself. Fruitless exercise. Not unlike masturbation, if you don't mind my saying."

"Not at all," the judge says, nodding vaguely, folding his paper and putting it in his jeans pocket. He laughs a little as he gazes at his new friend, then glances covertly at the cafeteria's exit.

KERBLAPSEE! Splikk! Fissszzzzzz. . . . . Scared the spunk right out of you, didn't I? Cats seldom receive credit for their sense of humour, but I venture to say that it is one of our greatest assets. If you tease us, we get it, do we not, and play along? Certainly we toy with you, whether you get it or not. Standing on your chest at three in the morning, our feet like frosted hypodermics penetrating your rib-cage to skewer your screaming vitals. Looking po'-faced for our food-dish when in exasperated surrender you're poised with spoon against plate to scrape its desiccated contents into the garbage. Yowling to be let out just when you're skittering for the washroom, your knees knocking. Biting your toes at four a.m., your naked and bloodless foot pinioned in our claws. Yum.

No, no one else has been electrocuted in the last twenty-four hours, or has even died of natural causes at Osgoode Hall — not to my knowledge, anyway. I was just staring off into space, as is the feline wont, into some other dimension, really, cogitating. (Katrina Slovenskaya has a cartoon tacked up on her cubicle, a cartoon from *The New Yorker* magazine which shows a cat staring at Stonehenge and thinking: *"I get it!"*) I was imagining, re-living, really, Jerry Debeers' final moments. Electrocution, they think it was. Not a pretty way to go, although in his case it seems to have been quick and clean. I once saw an electrocuted squirrel lying under the power lines outside the Dupont subway station. I learned from a quick study of the deceased that "fried" is no jocular euphemism in the more serious electrocution cases. All that remained was the unsuspecting creature's blackened skin, stretched like one of those beaver hides you see hung out to dry, as though the rodent had been flattened and eviscerated by a steamroller. But it was hairless and scorched into brittle squirrel-jerky, albeit of whole cloth, snout to paws, complete with little burnt-out ears and tiny blind eyesockets. Yes, the jolt had blasted the eyeballs clean out of its skull.

I've read in the library that the same thing happens to *Homo allegedly sapiens* in the electric chair. The blood boils. The brain sizzles. The eyeballs spring out of their cranial moorings like jacks-in-the-boxes onto the cheekbones. The skin blackens Cajun-style. Sometimes flames shoot out at the ears. Capital punishment. And they say *Homo sapiens* is the civilized species, distinguishing it from all other life forms on the planet.

Capital punishment. Funny phrase, that. *Capital* as in "the highest form," I suppose. But it's what people also say of good fortune and fortuitous events, of things worth having. *Capital assets. Capital gains. Capital goods. That's capital! Don't encroach on your capital.* Poor old Jerry Debeers. He was good and encroached upon. All liability, now. You'd need to have a real hate on for someone to do that to the fellow. Unpopular as the Splinter might have been, who would have decided that he merited capital punishment?

More to the point, who was willing to execute sentence of death in recompense, and only a few yards away from Her Majesty's higher law courts?

I wander into the benchers' library to find a detective — not Detective Sergeant Donovan, but a detective whose name-plate says Det. Insp. Yastremski — interviewing Treasurer Fitz-Niblick at the long cherry-wood table there. A constable sits with them, fiddling with his hat on the table.

"About this wine cellar log," the inspector is saying. "What do you suppose it might have been doing on the photocopier in the Journals Room?" He looks like a dog man, this Yastremski, all Polish sausage and pick-up hockey, obscurely angry as he shifts uncomfortably in the treasurer's oak guest chair, sweating pub pints if not buckets in the air-conditioned room. His clothing is two sizes too tight for the flesh spilling bloodless over the chair's edges, and his long-since broken nose causes him to breathe laboriously through his mouth, never mind that his mock-regimental tie remains uncinched, its knot failing miserably to hide the button on his unfastened collar.

Finicky Fitz-Niblick shrugs and shakes his head. "No idea, Inspector." He is not intimidated. The treasurer might be a small, portly man, but he is powerfully built for someone who spends his life at desks and committee dinners, and a man whose confidence and optimism are contagious and charming. He has a friendly mien, his forehead deeply lined with a manifest intelligence and inexhaustible cheerfulness. Every time I see him, even when he is dressed casually, he radiates elegance, trailing it after him by way of his expensive colognes and bath oils. His gold watch and wedding band are set off pleasantly, reassuringly, by his manicured fingernails and mocha skin, which always looks newly scrubbed and oiled. A man of detail, he speaks elegantly but slowly, sonorously, as though stoically oppressed, really, by having to keep it all up, this manifest burden of being an immigrant of colour in such fustian surroundings, where life-sized portraits of very dead white men — appeal justices and attorneys-general from a time when the only people of colour were escaped slaves at this particular terminus of the Underground Railroad — these Establishment WASPs gaze sternly over his shoulder everywhere he goes, except in the newer administrative and education wings, which have become showy tributes to contemporary multiculturalism. "It shouldn't have been there, I can tell you that. We keep it in the cellar, and it's regarded as strictly confidential."

"But why would that be? Isn't the cellar subsidized out of the members' fees?"

"Certainly. But that doesn't make it any less private. I mean, there are simply some quite valuable wines down there. You don't want to tempt pilfering, you know. Besides, our little cellar has been rather controversial over the years."

"How so, sir?" the constable asks.

"Well, number one, you also don't like to promote a public image of the profession's leaders as engaged in these sorts of wild bacchanals, wine, women, and song and all that sort of business." The treasurer laughs, throwing his head back to show his straight, stainless teeth to their maximum advantage. "If the public only knew how grim and tedious our work is, they'd hardly begrudge us the odd tipple."

"And number two, if there is one?"

"Well, we benchers do enjoy a glass of wine with our official dinners, you know, and really most of the rest of the profession never gets that opportunity. There's a little envy involved, you see, Inspector, never mind that any consumption is all very modest, and on formal occasions."

"Uh-huh. And would Mr. Debeers have been envious?"

"No. He could have imbibed along with the rest of us. He was teetotal, though, you see. So he would not have been envious at all. Not in the very least."

"But I understand that he didn't agree with having the cellar. Or serving the wine, anyway."

"Yes, that's right. He thought that, at least as far as the benchers' *consumption* was concerned, it should be stopped. But it didn't have anything to do with religion or teetotalling, I don't believe. He called it feudalistic, having a wine cellar, with us benchers being the lords of the manor, I suppose. Getting the gout and all that on the fleshpots of Egypt, in his view." Laughing again, the treasurer cocks his head and lowers his voice. "Jerry was more of the little-guy capitalist type, you know. A boot-straps democrat. Opportunity should knock on the doors of anyone who is righteous — that sort of thing. He thought we should sell the wine at auction or use it more generally, for the public, in the Barrister's Dining Room, and place the proceeds into general funds."

"Your operating funds."

"Precisely." The treasurer squints at Inspector Yastremski, as though really seeing him for the first time. "I'd be glad to offer you a glass of something." He smiles, spreading his handsome palms. "As I say, we do have some rather beautiful selections down there."

"And we'd be glad to accept," Yastremski chuffs, without returning the smile, "on another occasion, perhaps. But while we're on the subject, we'd like to have a quick look at your cellar after we're done here, if you wouldn't mind, sir." He hands Fitz-Niblick a piece of paper and asks, "Meanwhile, does any of this suggest anything to you?"

The treasurer re-cocks his head the other direction and studies the paper for a few seconds. "Couldn't say what it might mean, no." He jiggles his head amiably so that its silver pfitzer of hair glistens with some pleasantly scented gel, newly aromatic as he moves. "Couldn't say, I'm afraid." Yours Questingly hops up on the table and sits on the document, dumb and trying hard to look indifferent if not clueless. The part you can still see on the paper is handwritten in blue ink, and it says:

Fitz-Niblick — 30
Nobb — 30
Feldman — 15
Debeers $<$ *J — 15*
            A — 7
    E. T.? — 3

Half smiling, Fitz-Niblick queries, "Where did you get it, if I might ask?"

"Ms. Probert gave it to us," Yastremski replies. "She found it in Debeers' office, she says."

Fitz-Niblick pulls the paper out from under me and studies it again as he waves his other hand at my haunch and hisses *Scoot, scoot.* "Yes," he says distractedly, "Josey shared office space with Jerry up the street from here, near the newer temporary court building in that office tower." He looks up from the paper and adds, "Mind you, Mr. Nobb and I have been delegated to look after the winding up of his practice. So probably we should tell Josey not to shift things until we've had a look 'round the shop."

"She didn't know what that paper was, either," Inspector Yastremski says, reaching across the table to flick at the document with his sausage link of a finger. "But then, her name's not on it."

Fitz-Niblick shrugs and smiles at the staring officers, shaking his head. "I take your point, sir, but if that's me on there, I really couldn't say what the context would be. Beyond Law Society business, Jerry and I did not have a lot of truck with one another. Maybe he was totting up the prospective votes on some issue, some new motion he was going to make at convocation."

"We considered that. But we're told there's no bencher named Feldman."

Fitz-Niblick nods, looking extravagantly perplexed. "True enough. True enough."

"Do you know anything about a corporation he set up a couple of months ago, with his mother as a director? Did that come up in your trucking?" The detective manages a humourless smile.

"Can't tell you anything about that, either, I'm afraid." Fitz-

Niblick shrugs again. "He had his own practice and affairs. Again, we saw each other mostly on Law Society business, but that was it. We did not otherwise interact professionally, Inspector. And I can assure you that we did not socialize."

"His mother, Anika, Mrs. Debeers," the constable intervenes, "she says that she was just a small investor, and a director in name only. In this corporation, I mean." He is a pale man, with pale reddish hair. Compared to Fitz-Niblick, he looks like a ghost with malnutrition. He pushes at his hat, so that it squeaks against the high polish on the old table.

"Well, it's not uncommon for corporations to have nominal directors — directors who don't really have any real role or investment in the corporation. Sometimes the major shareholders don't want to have any particular managerial or public presence, themselves, so they put a child or a parent or someone like that in as director. That's quite common."

"Or their lawyer, I'm told," Yastremski adds.

"Or they put their lawyer in as director, certainly. Often. Doesn't mean a thing."

"So when she said that Jerry knew who the 'big enchiladas' were, that would have been other shareholders, in your opinion?"

"Well, in order for them to get long-term value out of the corporation, yes, they'd have to hold shares. Then again, the 'big enchiladas,' well, they could just be investors — you know, like lenders, someone who puts money in and gets paid interest on the loan. Like the company's bankers, say. Sometimes such investors are also named publicly as corporate officers. That way they try to make sure that they've got some control and oversight on the company's affairs, and on their investment. So the short answer is, yes, the shareholders are usually the big enchiladas. But not always, or not exclusively. And sometimes, yes, they're pretty well anonymous."

"Thank you, sir. Maybe we could see that cellar now?"

Stong Mariner is a four-year-old golden retriever who shares a comfortable two-storey, Tudor-style home in Upper Forest Hill Village with Theodore E. Mariner, His Lordship's wife, Penny, and their younger daughter, Claire, the semi-professional oboist. Stong's name comes, as you might have guessed, from the famous James Thurber essay, "How to Name a Dog." You will remember that Thurber spends just about all of the essay on how *not* to name your dog. Then, near the end, he tells the story of a dog-owner named Stong. Stong's dog looked something like the sadsack hounds "with long ears and troubled eyes" which Thurber drew for *The New Yorker*. That, Stong had explained to Thurber, was why he called his dog Thurber. So Thurber recommends that his readers call their dogs. . . .

Struggling daily under the weight of a literary joke for his name, Stong Mariner is a more than typical golden retriever. By this I mean that as far as harmless idiocy goes, he is the breed's quintessence. Big lugs, *Homo allegedly sapiens* is prone to call the typical golden; big lugs or dumb mutts. The golden species is celebrated for its mild temperament, but not, alas, for its intelligence. Stong Mariner's waking hours are one long series of meaning well but unerringly getting it wrong.

Now don't get your judicious correspondent wrong. There is no love lost between Stong Mariner and me, but neither is there any rush to judgment or pretrial bias on my part. Truly, I am as sober-minded in the matter as my judge, our mutual cross-species companion. And I am confident that His Lordship shares my view on Stong — which consensus can only help my case as the preferable companion animal. Consider the day that Stong comes to work with us as our reinforcement in the Squirrel Wars.

His Lordship introduces the enthusiastic mutt to an amenable young woman on the Osgoode Hall grounds crew. She is the sort who prefers animals to humans, which presumably makes her good in the garden as well, a favourite haunt of animals, companion and wild. As I have heard other Has-beings say, animals don't let you down, and probably the same can be said of nasturtiums and heliotropes. *He*, of course — Stong, I mean — is gormlessly delighted to make the young woman's acquaintance. He nearly throws his hind end through a nearby window and is only momentarily distracted from this new if characteristically fleeting ecstasy when His Lordship starts fiddling with his collar. Together, Justice Mariner and the gardener attach a sort of small boat hook to the deficient, if willing, cur. Knotted through the hook is a fair length of yellow nylon rope — enough that, in theory, Stong can pretty well patrol the outside radius of the entire stand of trees, scaring off rodent marauders. His Lordship ties the rope's other end to one of the apricot trees and wishes the gardener good luck. She has agreed to keep an eye on Stong and to make certain his water bowl is re-charged a couple of times during the day.

Of course, it doesn't take Stong more than two minutes to get his tether wound around a tree so that the squirrels disport themselves all about him in their private apricot Eden, ignoring the dog's inane, over-sized presence when they're not raining down dozens of stripped apricot halves on his foolish head. Occasionally he catches a jettisoned fruit-half in his mouth and swallows it down.

Later, just before lunch, I look out the window, and then I look again. I blink. I jump down from the window then immediately spring back up to check once more. I blink. I deliberately widen my pupils in that cat's way you Has-beings so envy and admire, so that my eyes blossom like black pansies in time-lapse photography. No, mine own poetic and miraculous eyes do not deceive me. Anchoring itself on its relatively strong hind legs, a plump brown squirrel — it looks a little like a youthful Fats Waller — cups an apricot half under its stumpy little forepaws, then shoots the ruined fruit into the air a couple of feet ahead. Stong chases the apricot down, carefully picks it up in his front teeth, and brings it undamaged back to the squirrel. Then he drops it at the squirrel's feet, and the game of fetch begins again.

Squirrels two, Mariners nil.

"Jeez," the constable says to Inspector Yastremski, "it's not as impressive as you'd expect, is it?" Then he turns to Fitz-Niblick. "I mean, not that much to look at, is it, sir?"

The constable's name, Fitz-Niblick now sees on his badge, is Pearce. "Not unless you know *what* you're looking at, constable," the treasurer replies, eyebrows up. "Welcome, gentlemen, to the fleshpots of Egypt."

True enough, the cellar is not much bigger than most living rooms, with a concrete floor and only narrow corridors for a body to navigate around its six rows of wood shelving, each crammed from ceiling to floor with the devil's own brew. To look at it, you would never know the cramped little room to be a potable Fort Knox.

"Nice and cool, though," the constable says. Damp, too, making me shiver for my blanket in the Humpty Dumpty potato chip box Marina has cut down for me and set next to her desk in the corner of the Reference Room.

"Yes, we keep it at about fifty-five degrees Fahrenheit all year round. That's the optimal standard. And as you can see, we organize everything by bin, according to varietal and vintage. Here, for instance, are the sherries. We serve them at convocation dinners, before the meal." Fitz-Niblick slides an Amontillado from a bin at waist height, gesturing with it at some boxes piled against the opposite wall. "And we just laid down about two hundred bottles of vintage port, which we serve after the main meal, with cheese and fruit or whatever, of course."

The policemen nod sagely, looking a little sick to their stomachs.

"But that particular batch — it won't be ready for another thirty or forty years. It's our gift to our successors, just as our forebears left us all this." The treasurer indicates the room generally, smiling with pride.

"Forty years is nothing. You'll just be reaching your prime by then," Inspector Yastremski attempts a joke, grinning weakly.

But the treasurer isn't listening. "Haven't even got it inventoried yet," he says, shaking his head in mock dismay. He waggles a coffee-coloured finger at the police officers. "Which is why we need that log back ASAP, guys."

"We'll have it back to you in plenty of time," the constable says, winking at his boss. "No more than thirty-nine years from today, for sure."

Fitz-Niblick remains in his own magic kingdom, mentally and physically. He has moved to a far corner of the little room, motioning at the officers with obvious glee. When we all join him he carefully fluffs half an inch of dust off the label on a bottle in this remotest and most shadowy bin. "This bottle you see here, gentlemen — take a good look. It's a rare, rare privilege, one of possibly five or six such bottles remaining in the entire world. If that many." I blink the dust from my eyes and sneeze. "Yes, gentlemen, a 1900 Château Margaux. Possibly the greatest vintage ever." His eyeglasses reflect the light of his admiration on the filthy love object. "And odds are, it's still *formidable*." Fitz-Niblick smacks his lips and shakes his head at the old wine in unbridled admiration. "After all these years — an entire century, gentlemen."

"And how much might that stuff go for?" the constable asks, nodding at the Margaux.

Fitz-Niblick shrugs. "Who knows, my dear young man? Who can say what this *stuff* might fetch. Thousands. Easily. Possibly ten." He lovingly slides the bottle back into the bin, careful not to disturb the sediment at its bottom, then claps his hands to clean them. "We also have a 1929 Mouton-Rothschild on hand that's nearly as precious. Not to mention a 1982 Pétrus that the Liquor Control Board is selling retail at four-thousand-five-hundred dollars these days. Which is why, as I've explained, we don't make a lot of noise about this modest little cellar of ours."

The treasurer grins like the Cheshire cat as the policemen stare back at him, apparently dumbfounded. "Thank you, Mr. Fitz-Niblick," Yastremski says at last, taking one final glance around the room and offering the treasurer his hand.

The treasurer walks his visitors to the cellar door. "So you've visited the mother, you say?" he asks the malnourished constable. "Mrs. Debeers, I mean. How is she taking all this, do you think?"

"Grimly," the constable replies.

"Noisily, anyway," the inspector corrects. "She's a bit of a tough old bird, rattling around in that house all by herself."

"Did you know that Mr. Debeers was a model train fanatic?" the pallid constable asks, smiling, his face showing some colour for the first time.

"I'd heard that, yes," Fitz-Niblick says, nodding and smiling vaguely.

"Takes up three-quarters of their basement," Inspector Yastremski says. "His mother paraded us down there to show us. It was the only time she cried." The detective smirks at the memory. "Then she started yelling at us again."

"It was incredible," the constable enthuses, suddenly animated, like a big kid. "Track set up with three or four different layouts, running around the whole basement. With little towns and farms and even model cattle and fences and water towers. You name it. My kids would've gone ape down there, I'll tell ya." He shakes his head in wonderment. "Hot as Hades down there, though. And humid like you wouldn't believe. Don't know how he could stand it."

"Not exactly a wine cellar," Yastremski agrees, rocking back on his heels. "More like a jungle."

"Basements," Fitz-Niblick says, seeming to exhaust his small talk.

"And get this," Yastremski adds, distracted by the memory.

"The old lady was still wearing a sweater. In June."

"You could've grown mushrooms down there," the constable says. "We could hardly breathe."

Fitz-Niblick ventures, "Old people feel the cold, I guess." Smirking, he hoists his hedgerow eyebrows two inches up his brown forehead and, all tickled at his newfound success in simple-minded banter, forgets to lower them. He shifts his considerable bulk, though, obviously more comfortable with less folksy topics such as the personal liability of estate trustees or the remedies of secured creditors under the *Companies Creditors Arrangement Act*. Or maybe he's just feeling his age, himself, and all that weight of being treasurer of the Law Society of Upper Canada in this white man's waspish world. I can see it quite plainly in his expensively shod feet. What the lips say, body language at Gucci-level can deny. (With *felis sylvestris* ambling around at shin level, you should mind the tongue in your shoe, too.) "The mother, I mean."

"I guess," the constable says, waving, his smile fading. "Take care, then, sir."

CHAPTER 5

Reasonable and Probable Grounds

My own mother, for what it's worth, did not live to enjoy or lament her old age. The fact that I was orphaned to live in the streets has afforded me a certain sympathy, or at least an abiding empathy, for what some thoughtlessly call the criminal and under-classes. *There but for the grace of God go I,* and you, too, I often think. All the best lawyers feel this in their bones, I believe, prosecution and defence side both. It's the Law, after all, by which I mean the laws of nature, which inform the small l law and every-thing else in your *Homo allegedly sapiens* world-view. For me, all of criminal law is summed up in Newton's Third Law of Motion: To every action there is an equal and opposite reaction. Or, as Freud put it in the human context, the good cop got that way by resist-ing his darkest killer impulses. The same goes, of course, for the most serious puritans, like John Calvin, Oliver Cromwell, and Jeremiah "the Splinter" Debeers.

Me, I was born in that alleyway just west of Levy's Deli in Kensington Market, an alley behind a row of conjoined two-storey buildings — an old strip mall, so-called. On the ground floor were a dry cleaner's, a Pizza Pizza, a luggage repair shop, a Polish bakery, an optometrist, a watch-repair shop, the deli. . . . Above were apartments and flats, cramped, noisy, dusty, pollution-oppressed. You can imagine the flyblown air and pavement pungent with concatenated motor vehicle exhaust and spilled engine oil, the perfume of sourdough, ethanol, salami, burnt pepperoni and overcooked tomato sauce, spilled booze and vomit and urine and cola, the comestible refuse dumped out back, a real smorgasbord for vermin and street life, which naturally is why Mother chose the spot to shelter her third or fourth or fifth litter, whichever we might have been.

I remember her only vaguely, of course, black like me, but mottled salt and peppery — *glory be to God for dappled things* — on her ears, her left haunch, and across the right side of her nose, something like a hunting hound. It made her exotic to would-be mates and Has-beings alike, I believe. One morning she dutifully went out looking for a mouse, rat, or unfortunate starling to bring back alive to train us on, for it was that time in our lives. The moment to scorn sentiment had come for all of us, including Mother. But she never experienced that bittersweet luxury. She was run over, twice, I later heard, by a delivery truck outside the bakery. And, carrying around one or the other of us mewling waifs to make the case, begging, cajoling, and looking very sad on her own account before the optometrist, pizza boys, luggage repairman, et. al., the woman who ran the bakery with her husband distributed us to whomever would take us in — customers, neighbours, fellow shopowners.

That was how I ended up at Levys', contemplating Newton's Third Law of Motion.

⁌ை⁍

In adulthood, anyway, we are all waifs, nostalgic for the time when somebody else looked after us and all our childish fears. This occurs to me as I gaze now at poor Katrina. I can sense that she is petrified. It is her turn for the obligatory police interview. Having introduced themselves, Detectives Donovan and Yastremski sit opposite her, crowd her from both sides of escape in her cell-like cubicle, never mind that it's in a fairly public area, near the Duck Blind. She has been rigid with nerves about the questioning all morning, and I suppose we both feel some relief that the time has come to get it done and dusted. Notoriously, the worst thing about punishment is the waiting. I have tried to reassure her, tacitly, that the interview is a mere formality, just part of routine police work. But she is entitled to counsel, of course, so I vault onto the desk and take my place at her right hand, or shoulder, never forgetting that she did the same for me that fateful day before Mr. Justice Mariner in the front courtyard.

"Anika Debeers tells us that you had business dealings with Jerry," Detective Donovan is saying.

What's this? Run a business? Katrina? She couldn't run water from her kitchen tap.

"Who's Anika Debeers?" she asks, half smiling.

Good girl. Keep 'em on their toes.

"Jerry's mother. Are you saying you don't know her?"

"Oh, yes, Mrs. Debeers. Of course. His mother. He mentioned her. I've never met her, really. Just said hello one time. I mean, I didn't know Jerry that well. A little, I mean. Not well."

"Not well. Yet you're a co-director with his mother of this numbered company that he set up for her? And you've never met her?"

The iron-eyed lady detective hands Katrina a piece of paper.

"ARTICLES OF INCORPORATION," it says, at the top. "1. The Name of the corporation is |1|2|5|3|2|1|4| |O|N|T|A|R|I|O| |L|I|M|I|T|E|D|."

"And the business address printed there is your apartment, isn't it?" Inspector Yastremski says, a little too loudly for a library, if you ask me.

Don't answer that, I tell Katrina. Not that I think she has anything to hide. I just want to know what they're getting at first. As I say, this Yastremski has the look and savour of a hardhead who keeps Rottweilers.

"Oh, that." Katrina laughs nervously. I mew quietly, insinuatingly, and lean against her. *Blame me. I'll take the heat for ya, darlin', then exercise my gypsy prerogative to flee the court's jurisdiction. Have not history and The Law themselves chosen the role of scapecat for me?* "It's my house, actually. One side of a semi. I own it with my sister." She looks at the paper and laughs again, then looks pleadingly at the cops. "I was just helping out. Jerry said that it was only a formality. That lawyers sometimes put themselves down as directors of their clients' companies, but, because it was his mother and he was a bencher, well, he thought it was better just to keep himself out of it, in case the company, you know, in case it got complicated."

The detectives look at her for what seems like a week. So she giggles. "I mean, it wouldn't look good if a bencher's mother had a company and it went belly up or something, I guess." *Shah!* I say. They think I'm coughing up a hairball, no doubt. Katrina shrugs. "That's how Jerry explained it, anyway."

"And what did this corporation do?" Yastremski asks.

"I'm not completely sure."

"You're a director and you don't know?"

"Well, I think it was real estate development. You know, some kind of properties. His mother's investments, and maybe his, I guess. I'm not sure. I was just doing them a favour."

"As you probably understand, we have to ask people about their movements on the night Mr. Debeers died. Can you tell us where you were on Sunday, June the eighth, in the evening, between six and eight o'clock, say?"

"Well, normally I would be at home. But that evening I was here until a little after six. I was going out to dinner with a friend."

"Can your friend verify that?"

"Yes, I would think so."

"Who's your friend, then, Katrina? And where can we find him or her?"

"Her. It's Josey — Josey Probert. She's another bencher. A friend of Jerry's. And mine, of course." Katrina giggles again. "So, you can find her . . . well, here, I guess. Or at her law office."

"Oh, yes," Sergeant Donovan says, flipping through her notebook. "She's on our contact list."

Bored now, I jump down to the floor and nose around the coppers' feet.

"So you left at about what, six?"

"A little after. Maybe almost six-thirty. We got to talking and we were running late."

"Talking where?"

I notice that the bottom drawer in Katrina's desk is open a little, and I can smell that cold pizza — with pepperoni, green olives, and roasted red peppers, if I'm not mistaken — might still be in there, left over from her dinner and then today's lunch. The metal drawer is on little rubber wheels, so it's no trick to widen the opening for a good nosey around. I do it all the time, of course, just to keep tabs. I stick a paw in the gap and pull.

"Here, in the library. We're open until five p.m. on Sundays."

"Was anyone else around?"

"You mean when I left?"

The sergeant nods. The drawer doesn't give, so I paw more vigorously.

"As far as I know, no one. I mean, we were already closed. It's usually pretty quiet in here on the weekends, anyway, although you generally get a couple of people up until closing. I had my mystery book with me — I like the old Dorothy Sayers', the old-style detective stories. And Simenon. Maigret." *Giggle.* "There are lots of them — a steady supply, you know. Anyway, you don't care about that, I don't suppose. I mean, I was just waiting for Josey to finish some bencher business. Reading while I waited."

"So is that why you were in the library? Just waiting?"

"Well, I have a key, of course." Inspector Yastremski arches his eyebrows to indicate there is no of course about it. "It just made sense to wait here."

"And you met Josey Probert here?"

"Yes, she came here. We met here, I mean."

"And did you come back here again that night at all?"

Before Katrina can answer, I manage to get my claws stuck in the lip of the drawer-front, where it curls back on itself. I twist right, twist left, right left right left, testing the full flexibility of my feline sinews as the drawer pulls farther and farther out of Katrina's desk without letting go of Yours Inquisitively. When it reaches the brake on the back panel, I admit it, I panic. I can't help it. I start to thrash and yowl and mewl like a kitten. *Help! The monster's got me and it won't let go. It's going to gobble me up alive, along with last year's Christmas party announcement, a furry cough lozenge, and the vacation days roster I can see in its guts at the back of the desk!* Anyway, I get a little exuberant about it, I guess, because before I know it the whole bloody desk begins pitching forward under the burden of the drawer's contents and my desperate exertions. Supporting the desk's full weight, the runners on the pulled-out drawer give up the ghost with a crack like a gunshot BANG!, and then another BANG!, and another BANG!, and then the whole bloody unit just about overbalances onto poor, soft Katrina and Yours Nearly Pulverized. Talk about your third degree.

Happily, that particular disaster is averted by the two visiting coppers, who right the desk and kick at the broken drawer. But then, suddenly, everybody is staring — check that: *gawping* — at the drawer's contents, now so boisterously exposed to plain view. It's not Katrina's lunch bag crumpled up in the front that's got our attention. It's what's just behind it, plain as day, now, in the fluorescent glare of the room. We all goggle, mouths agape, at a little Tupperware box sitting in its own top. Neatly packed inside the box we note:

    one pair of Mastercraft wire strippers;
    one Mastercraft steel wire cutter;
    sundry grades of copper wiring, insulated and non-;
    one roll of black electrical tape;
    and one half-sheet of crumpled and greasy aluminum foil.

Judicial Interim Release (Out on Bail)

"The old joke has it that, come August, the world is even crazier than usual. August, of course, is when all the psychotherapists go on vacation. In compensation, perhaps, the world is a little more just in August, as well. For August is also when the courts close down for the judges' annual retreat."

In those words the Chief Justice welcomes some 335 judges to the Fool's Rush Inn in Gotham, on the shores of Lake Chelmsford in the Muskoka Lakes region, about three hours north of the city. The conferees laugh and applaud, a little nervous in all this open space and natural light, light-headed on the ripe country air, not quite relaxed, queasy, delirious, like schoolchildren on the first day of camp. I can hear the Welcome Dinner festivities quite clearly through the thin walls, intensifying my migraine times ten, never mind that I am shut up in a humid room three doors down from the dining hall. The inn is redolent of cedar and pine needles, a truly torturous stink to the refined sensibilities of *felix urbanus*, who prefers the perfume of the abattoir and fish market. Katrina, of course, is indisposed. The Great Library is running on skeleton staff until Labour Day, Leland Gaunt is visiting his parents in

Saskatchewan, and Justice Theodore Mariner is, to quote his very hurtful phrase, "saddled with that damn *Adversarius Curiae* again." That's Enemy of the Court, in case your Latin's not quite up to thoughtless abuse. Lovely.

Apparently I am become an albatross around the ancient Mariner's neck. But who, exactly, is saddled with whom, I ask you: the *Homo allegedly sapiens* who drove up here for five nights of plastic potato salad and seminars on "Regional Case Management" and "Jury Challenges in the New Millennium," or the *felis sylvestris* who was collared by court security and gaoled in a carrier two sizes too small, then black Maria-ed into the wilderness for three hours in the back of His Lordship's smelly old Volvo paddy wagon, itself in desperate need of new suspension and piston valve rings? *Cruel and unusual punishment!* I howled it the whole way here by way of an application under the *Charter of Rights and Freedoms, 1982*, getting nothing but a blanket thrown over my carrier for an answer, not counting the occasional curse and dire threat or imprecation cast my direction.

Bunking down at the Mariner home was out, you see, because Claire the oboist daughter is allergic. Mind you, to his credit, our eructing passenger, Dylan Faddaster of the *Daily Standard*, was rather more sympathetic than His Lordship. "The poor little guy," he kept saying, and thanks to the six bathroom stops he requested, we periodically got a little fresh air into the old Volvo wagon. Even for the journey Faddaster wore a suit that was about one-point-five sizes too small for him, a tie pulled askew from his dishevelled collar, and a stained white shirt unbuttoned from mid-chest up, showing his hairless white bosom blotched with patches of sickly pink. As he offered around his little bag of salted nuts he sweated profusely, so that you couldn't tell if it was perspiration or peanut oil on the sack, never mind that the air conditioner was on full blast, the only setting still available. It felt like February to Yours Hypothermically. But Faddaster is a stereotype if not an archetype, a throwback: the journalist of big appetites but also of tender heart.

"Had this damn bug for several weeks now," he has confessed, unapologetically, failing to cover his mouth even once as he spluttered and coughed the whole way up to Gotham. "Can't seem to shake it." It was true. Consider how in hospitals you can smell the carnal decay through all that bleach and Lysol. Likewise, sniffing through the bars of the carrier, pricking up my ears (you do that a lot in prison), I could detect Faddaster's liver, as well as several other vital organs, no doubt, begging for mercy through a cloud of his mint-flavoured mouthwash.

Ah, entropy. There's a lot of it around these days, putrid and prickly even through the humid pine-needles and cedar. Now, anyway, as my own brain bangs against my skull so that my eyes throb and my poor belly convulses from residual car sickness, Faddaster is being vociferously ill into the toilet next door while the Chief Justice sonorously tells his jokes three doors down in the other direction. Poor us. "They say that more fools pass through Gotham than remain in it," the chief booms through his microphone, recalling the town's legendary namesake, whose wise fools feigned idiocy to discourage King John from building an estate in their midst while taxing them for the cost. "But actually, I think it's the golf course here that really separates the buffoons from the wise — those folks who just head for the beach with a good book." Highly risible.

I suppose this lakeside resort is quite lovely, if you share the

Has-beings' taste for manicured nature. Besides the serviceability of the town's name in after-dinner speeches, and a golf course that in fact flatters the player's abilities, Gotham boasts huge muskenonge, walleye, pickerel, and trout in a large, albeit human-made, freshwater lake, as well as many of the biggest fish in the legal community among its seasonal cottagers. And then there is the Fool's Rush Inn.

Inevitably, they dress the poor bellboys as jesters and instruct them to zap you with buzzers when they shake your hand in greeting. When you sit in the lounge or dining room, the cushion beneath you is likely to erupt in loud flutterings, as of startled pigeons. The cabana boys will squirt you with giant water guns, and even the waitresses are "themed" as "serving wenches," though they are more often post-menopausal than nubile; fleshy, red-faced, and all sweaty in yards of stiff fabric, they remind you of the sclerotic peasant women in paintings by Breughel as they gamely go through their thankless labours. The strain takes its toll, of course. When we first arrived and His Lordship ordered a pizza to share with some colleagues in our room, the "wench" who brought it to the door, a plump townswoman with badly bleached hair and false teeth, showed him a deadened smile and asked: "Did you hear about the Zen Buddhist who said to the pizza man: 'Make me one with everything'?" When one of the other judges ordered a pitcher of draft beer, the poor woman blinked, then spouted from her store of gags: "What do alcoholics call New Year's Eve?" Dylan Faddaster ruined that one, mind you, by holding up his finger and shouting, "Amateur night."

⁊ᴔᴑ

Feeling better, apparently, having forgone the welcome dinner, Faddaster takes the air on the walkway just outside our rooms. Ducking under the window curtains in the suite I share with the judge, and using the curtains as a ladder to the inside ledge, I can see the beleaguered journalist looking out over the lake. Taking a breather from the dinner, Treasurer Fitz-Niblick joins him, smoking a cigar. "You're looking a little green around the gills these days, old chum," he says, "if you don't mind my saying."

Faddaster squeezes the bridge of his nose, shakes his head, and flexes his neck. "Hell, Sammy, I've even been peeing green, when I'm not seeing it. My bowels are in permanent uproar these days."

No doubt Nobb would have replied that he always knew Faddaster was full of it. Fitz-Niblick chuckles and puffs at his cigar, considering the journalist through the blue haze this sets up as the moths and mosquitoes buzz around Faddaster. At last the treasurer takes a more indirect approach: "But it's second nature with you, anyway, isn't it, Faddy, raising a stink?"

"It's no joke. I've been bloody sick. For weeks, now."

"Doesn't interfere with the muckraking, though, I take it."

"Hey, as long as you're making it, Sammy, I'm raking it."

"You've raked hard enough, Dylan." *Puff puff.* "I'll give you that." *Puff.* "Turned over just about every rock in the garden. But name me one thing that's stuck during my tenure as treasurer. All the muck that's never stuck. That's your motto, eh?" *Puff puff.*

"Come on, Sammy. I know you're one of my most devoted readers."

"Keeping mine enemy closer than my friends, old friend, or however it goes. Keeping you where I can watch you, Dylan, old boy."

Faddaster shakes his head. "You know, I'm always getting that stuff, about how awful the tabloids are, how sensationalist. I have to laugh. People hate sensationalism so much that this country supports a dozen tabs full of sex and scandal and diet fads. We're so unpopular we keep all the publishers in champagne and German luxury cars." He chuffs, rubbing his eyes and yawning. "Meanwhile, I'm just a galley slave to it all — an underpaid public servant, just like you, Sammy, except you're as rich as the sultan of Brunei. Her Majesty's press." Faddaster smiles and bows. "At your public service."

"You're sounding a little defensive, old chum." Fitz-Niblick puffs away.

"And your cigar stinks like shit. You'll have me puking again."

An old hand at ignoring crudity, Fitz-Niblick is unfazed. Blowing smoke in Faddaster's general direction, he says, "Anyway, tell me all about the latest diet fad. Both of us could give it a try, I would think. Hmm?" Here, the treasurer pats his Toby-jug belly with a proprietary air as he nods at Faddaster's painfully distended gut.

Faddaster grimaces in pain, as though the treasurer has punched him there. "Hey, don't laugh. In a sense, the whole world's united by dieting, you know. Global village and all that." He yawns again, then coughs. "One half's on your Hollywood doctor's high protein, low carb regime while the other half fucking starves. So don't tell me we don't print legitimate issues of the day. I mean, we're all on a slimming plan, voluntarily or not. Give pizza a chance, I say, sir." Faddaster pauses to take a swig straight from the little bottle of whatever forty-proof painkiller he has liberated from the bar in his room. Then he winces and assumes a confidential tone. "Speaking of which. Now that Debeers has bought the farm, I guess you can go ahead and privatize the dining operation at Osgoode Hall. It's a done deal, right? The opposition's eliminated, more or less?"

Fitz-Niblick smiles broadly, shaking his head. "Ah. Never off duty, are we, Dylan?"

"Can't afford to be, Sammy. But, no kidding. It's a go, right? The privatization. Between you and me."

"Why do you ask? Thinking of putting in a bid, yourself?"

"You never know your luck."

The treasurer laughs softly. "*You* never know yours, my friend. But luck is something I personally never depend upon. You should remember that about me. I can't afford to depend on luck, either."

Faddaster sighs. "Neither could poor old Jerry, I guess."

"And may he rest in peace, too," the treasurer adds, with a little bow of his own.

After lunch the next afternoon, a team of scrawny, unsunned Crowns in cutoffs and bathing suits takes on a similarly clad motley of mostly overweight judges at beach volleyball. The Near-Sighted Hangashores against the Beached and Bloating Whales, you might say. On the theory that discretion is the better part of valour, Justice Mariner sits the contest out at a nearby picnic table, wearing his Panama hat and sandals, engrossing himself in a book called *Ardor in the Court!: Sex and the Law* — rather a busman's holiday, it seems to Yours Critically. But that must remain his own judicious business. It is time, I am afraid, to leave him to his own devices, to cut, as it were, the *Amicus umbilicus*. The maid has left the door ajar, and I have more or less spontaneously determined to make good my escape. Opportunity, as Treasurer Fitz-Niblick no doubt would agree, is there to be seized.

As you know, my days with His Lordship have been profitable enough, comfortable and productive, even, if I say so myself. But apparently I have outlived my usefulness and the Doghouse on River Street is my immediate future. *I am become an albatross around the ancient Mariner's neck.* And anyway I weary once more of these various imprisonments and prior restraints at the hands of *Homo allegedly sapiens* and its purported civilization. *I cannot rest from travel.* . . . It is time to free myself from this never-ending probation order of domestication, this anthropocentric universe of might is right.

I cannot rest from travel; I will drink
Life to the lees . . .

While most of the conferees are preoccupied with sunning, chatting, conventioneer flirting, and weekend-jock volleyball, I trot nonchalantly onto the beach and then along the shoreline of Lake Chelmsford, toward the periphery of Gotham proper.

For always roaming with a hungry heart
Much have I seen and known — cities . . .

Unfortunately, before long I am nobbled by none other than Leland Gaunt, chambers' official nebbish, already blatantly playing the traitor as a member for the Crown side at volleyball.

"Judge!" the scrawny clerk hollers, wheezing from his clumsy, treasonous exertions for the prosecution. "Judge! It's the bloody cat again. He's going AWOL on you." He'll pay for this, one way or another. I note with satisfaction that his nose and arms are already sunburned, quite horribly.

"Bloody hell," His Lordship mutters, tearing himself away

from his *Ardor in the Court,* setting it down in spilled iced tea on its spread-eagled pages as he stands and shades his eyes to have a look at my retreating fanny.

"Don't worry. He'll wander on back when he's hungry," another judge negligently advises.

"Hey, this is farm country," Gaunt says. "A fox or bear'll get him if we don't." He rubs his belly, pasty and concave above his swim trunks. "Everything's hungry in this air." He belches, making the mole above his navel jump.

"'Specially for a little pampered delicacy trucked in from the city," His Lordship mutters.

And so the chase is on, until I am semi-encircled, on the dry land side, by various officers of the court in various states of undress, sunstroke, and general physical disrepair, all of them panting and unhealthily pallid. *I am become a name.* There is nothing for it but to take to sea.

You should know that it is utter human nonsense that *felis sylvestris* as a species is unable to swim. There are well-documented cases, you can check them out, of cats deliberately diving into lakes and ponds to fish. Then again, as a creature of your more intellectual inclinations, a feline who is learned, after all, in the law, I personally am not especially gifted, aquatically speaking. Things start off all right enough, with a bit of the old dog paddle, so to say, but then the sand-and-rock bottom suddenly drops completely away from my hind paws. My nose and ears fill with the ice-cold and metallic *aqueous vitae* — or, imminently it would seem, *aqueous obiti.* Death by water. Paddling furiously, I am able to bob to the surface, only to sink ignominiously one-point-three seconds later, my head festooned with weeds and slime. Of course I have heard on television (produced quite obviously by *Homo absolutely unsapiens)*, on some cartoon show, no doubt (yes, possibly "Sylvester the Cat and Tweetie Bird," yes, highly amusing, yes), that it's three times under and you're gone. Water is already in the lungs, and as I surface again I sputter in that diminutive, heart-rending way of the sneezing housecat. My entire habitually silken coat is covered now with slime and vegetation, greasy dun weeds draped over my poor ears and snout. Then, sodden with misery, I am under for the final chapter. Adieu, dear Mariner. Goodbye, cruel world. This particular story shall finish without me, no doubt, and my ninth life.

Before long, I stop flailing about. There is no point, after all, and really it is lovely-quiet under here, tranquil and dreamy. Just when I am resigning myself to the peace of it, there is a not-peace, a churning all about me, and the water is suddenly aerated with muddy little green bubbles, prickling at my belly, lifting at my forelegs. A very large Has-being head barks my jaw. My tongue tastes of metal, quicksilver, as though poisonous mercury were leeching into my skull out of my rattled, bruised eyes and nostrils. I feel the sleep of surrender on me again, as though in a surprised but not displeased way I am homeward bound, free at last. But then something else, not just the bubbles, but Has-being fingers, claw at my armpit, squeeze the remaining air out of me, and pull me upwards. Both of us gasping and choking, Dylan Faddaster and I break the surface of the bilious lake, then sink yet again. He clasps me to his formerly white dress shirt, now plastered against his whale-like flesh. Through the weeds on my eyes, I can see that he still wears that dirty, undersized suit and his loosened tie. We make quite a pair, it occurs to me groggily, humorously — something out of a movie by Luis Buñuel, or maybe Fellini.

I slip from his clumsy grasp and it looks like we're both goners for sure. With that thought the fear slows anew. Unlike *Homo allegedly sapiens* generally, the rest of the animal world knows how and when to make its peace with death. I begin to feel analytical, bemused, reassured; the stillness of it all, the aloneness, seems to clarify everything, and, paradoxically, to make me ardent to resume my work at Osgoode Hall. I seem to comprehend for the first time, or to be reborn in the concept, that I, Questing Cat, am called to unfinished business. My quest. Mine own crusade and Renaissance. *What will become of Katrina Slovenskaya, fair maiden?* I keen. Anyway, it seems to be taking much longer to die than I would have predicted, when unexpectedly the sand is back under my hind legs. My head and chest, Dylan Faddaster's head, chest, thighs, knees, are above water. Staggering, coughing, spitting, not quite believing it, we find that we are near the shore and each of us can stand. *It's a miracle!* Felliniesque, bleary-eyed, sobbing, falling over one another, we stumble toward the trees beyond the beach. The water runs in rivulets off Faddaster's ruined suit and squirshes from his black dress shoes with every lumbering, stumbling step. We are saved. There must be a reason.

By now a bigger crowd has gathered on the shore, a blurry, cheering rabble in which several judges of the Superior Court and Court of Appeal figure prominently, even through seaweed. Justice Mariner, looking genuinely worried, bless him, throws his head back at the heavens, so that his Panama hat falls behind him onto the sand. He shakes his hands before him in mingled frustration and relief, like Job in the middle of his trials. Finally, he shakes his head and laughs. "What d'ya know!" he shouts at fat and choking Dylan Faddaster, who is being violently ill in the trees. "Faddaster for the little guy, yet again." Never has the journalist been so popular.

Miriam Belgrade, Assistant Crown Attorney in the Newmarket Superior Court, towels me dry and cleans the weeds from my coat as I shiver away, gagging silently under the warm cotton, grimly expecting dysentery as my holiday souvenir, soundlessly praying for my home, fanatasizing that I am snug in my corner of the Reference Room in the Great Library at Osgoode Hall, warm and dry in my Humpty Dumpty box with my belly full of Katrina's relatively digestible tuna salad sandwiches. I blink as the towel comes off my head, then close my eyes against the sunlight. *Is this Heaven,* I find myself asking Miriam Belgrade, *or is it Hell?*

"The trouble is," Faddaster interrupts, as he limps over, coughing, and someone hands him a towel, "I can't fucking swim, either."

PART TWO

Judgment

CHAPTER 1

Off the Record

The prosecution of *Her Majesty the Queen against Katrina Daniella Slovenskaya* has taken an unpromising turn for the assistant librarian charged with first-degree murder. We are well into the Crown's case. Anika Debeers has been in the witness box since 9:30, and as court opens after the morning break, Katrina's lawyer is suddenly on his hind legs begging, and I mean *begging*, Madam Justice Hossanah M'Gonnigle to let him out of representing the accused Ms. Slovenskaya. Roman Nobb, Q.C., lapped up the assignment eagerly enough the morning Mr. Justice Mariner and I telephoned him from chambers these many months back. When His Lordship said, "I can't believe she'd do anything of the sort, Roman" (and I helpfully added, *Wouldn't hurt a mouse)*, Nobb was all old-boy jolly jokes and condescending reassurance from that Parnassus inhabited by Life's Chosen: "Don't sweat it, Ted. We'll make sure she gets what's coming to her." His Lordship crinkled his nose at me in disgust. Nothing like sucking up to a judge of the Court of Appeal.

Later that day Katrina called us from the Don Jail, where she was a conscripted guest of Her Majesty. According to what His

Lordship told her, Nobb might not be the King of Torts, but he certainly is the prince of society-page litigation. He fancies himself a Clarence Darrow or Perry Mason type, Justice Mariner warned the librarian. "You know, he said, "the old-fashioned orator-advocate who persuades the court with his alleged wit and wisdom more than on the law, about which he usually has little or no idea." Hiring Nobb was, in other words, "like all high pay-off investments, a calculated crap shoot. From the bench, you often wonder where the Sam Hill he's going, and he often seems to wonder the same thing himself." Although Katrina couldn't see him, His Lordship shook his head. "You notice he'll always have a junior along with him in court, to get him back on the rails. Watch out for that look of panic that suddenly hits him when the judge asks a question. That's why I'll be lending him my clerk, Leland, to pull old Nobb back on the straight and narrow and keep me in the picture at the same time."

Nobb's more usual beat these days was commercial litigation, particularly if there was old money involved, with its promise of dependable fees that he could cream off the top in inflated retainers. Typically, he handled estate disputes (often on referral from Fitz-Niblick), shareholder battles in family or other closely held (and frequently dodgy) companies, some medical malpractice and other personal injury cases, and the occasional high-society divorce. But like Justice Mariner, he'd earned his barrister's spurs under the old British-style system in which the trial lawyer is popularly characterized as a hackney, circling the inns of court and duty-bound to pick up any prospective litigant who flags him down from the pavement. When Nobb began his legal career, those litigants were very often criminals waving legal aid certificates at duty counsel sitting across the courtroom, waiting for any file with a fee. So he had some experience of the criminal courts, stale-dated though it was. And in his view, a trial lawyer was a trial lawyer, never mind the issues in dispute.

"The thing is, Katrina, Roman's legend precedes him, see?" my companion human added. Holding a rather more temperate view than Nobb did of the barrister's calling — one might say a more judicious view, with a mind-set less focused on milking every file for its cream — His Lordship had specialized in criminal defence practice, eventually, plying that side of the street for twenty-two years before his move to the trial court bench. "He's lived a charmed life, and it's infectious. I think that's an advantage to you in a case where the circumstantial evidence is pretty strongly against you. Especially before an old-fashioned judge like M'Gonnigle. The judges, at least the older ones, are all a little afraid of Mr. Nobb. They think they're the ones who are confused, when it's just as likely it's Roman whose wandering around in the thickets, looking for the trail he's somehow lost. But don't be alarmed by that. Leland'll be there to show him the way back, and on balance, I'd say Roman's good for your case. Leland'll keep me up to date, and together we'll make a formidable team."

But at this moment Nobb is anything but formidable. Having made my way to the courthouse at 361 University, through that underground tunnel connecting it to the Hall, and having settled in comfortably at the feet of the dictaphone stenographer, I can see sweat glistening on the old Q.C.'s forehead under his carefully combed mane of white hair. He licks his lips repeatedly. His collar and the tops of his tabs and gown are wet with perspiration. He is, not to put too fine a point on it, green around the usually ruddy-skinned, Anglo-Saxon gills. He grips his robing bag — which with age is the colour of dried blood — by its dirty golden draw string as though he is ready to run out of the room, or more likely, as a way of telegraphing to the judge that his request to withdraw from the record is a *fait accompli* and, considering that he is a bencher and senior member of the litigation bar, he refuses to hear otherwise. You can see the outline of his *Martin's Annotated Criminal Code* in the robe bag when you would expect less brazen counsel to have it prominently before him on the desk, just in case — just as Crown counsel, Gordon Mortimer, has his open there to section 231:

> *(1) Murder is first degree murder or second degree murder.*
> *(2) Murder is first degree murder when it is planned and deliberate. . . .*

But Her Ladyship (or, as Nobb calls her, falling in with the modern way, given his circumstances, Her Honour) is having none of it. "Mr. Nobb," she is saying, glaring at him over the black plastic bar on her otherwise rimless eyeglasses ("It looks like a designer Cro-Magnon eyebrow that keeps falling down her face," I heard Nobb whisper to his junior, Leland Gaunt, sitting behind him, "so I call her Groucho of 361"), "you have yet to give me a good, or *any* reason, for that matter, to permit you to abandon ship mid-trial like this, after we've heard all the pre-trial motions not to mention your opening, the Crown's opening, and after the Crown has already called two witnesses. I have a scrap of paper in front of me, yes, but it doesn't show me that you're in any conflict of interest regarding this particular matter, a murder trial. Does it? I just don't get it, Mr. Nobb. Hmm?"

The jury and witness have been dismissed so as not to hear this colloquy, and Her Honour is quite red in the face. Otherwise, she is mostly elegant, all right, and hardly Cro-Magnon at all. Tall and lithe, looking a little like a dancer even in her robes, her grey eyes — which match the silvery-grey streaks of her chestnut-brown hair — are lively as they engage counsel and court staff, her movements impressively quick and decisive. Feline, you might say.

"Well, Your Honour," Nobb gabbles, his charm not quite in play as his movie star baby-blues shift here and there looking for a way out, "as I've explained, for fear of compromising the defence and the solicitor-client privilege existing between my client Ms. Slovenskaya and myself, I can't really say much more. As I've explained earlier, it's only just come to my attention that it's not feasible for me to continue here as trial counsel. I really am in a potential conflict situation, you see, Your Honour."

From outside, you can hear Ernie the Evangelist, quoting Jeremiah again over his squawk-horn: *And it shall come to pass-a when ye shall say-a, Wherefore doeth the Lord our God-a these things unto us-a?*

"No, frankly, I don't. You keep saying that, but if you're not going to elaborate, how can I see anything, Mr. Nobb? All I see is fog. Fog and hot air." The judge throws her hands up in exasperation.

"Well, I apologize for that, Your Honour, but I can't be clearer. That's the whole point. And my colleague Mr. Gaunt here is in a perfectly good position to carry on in my place, or to instruct other senior counsel to do so. So there's no prejudice to the client at all."

The client. He's already disowned poor Katrina.

That unfortunate worthy, by the way, she of the house-cat named for the witches' demonic familiar, sits penned in the dock, looking confused, crushed, and alone, very much like the last standing babushka doll after the bull has left the china shop. *Double, double, toil and trouble. Fire burn and cauldron bubble.* Sniffing the torch fires of a witch hunt, I'm afraid I mewl aloud, putting myself at risk of being turfed out — which is no less than I deserve, I suddenly feel, hanging my head, ashamed that I dropped her in it with that desk drawer incident. *Me, a nark, a fink, a stoolie? Not guilty, m'Lady, you gotta believe me. Would I grass up Katrina Daniella Slovenskaya, my dearest friend — at least when Mr. Justice Mariner isn't, or Elise Throckmorton or Modesto the sous-chef in the Barrister's Dining Room or a passing bar admission student or the cleaners or the kitchen staff or Johnny the homeless guy who sits near Ernie the Evangelist playing the harmonica very badly for change just outside the cowgates on University and with his filthy fingertips tries to feed me crumbs from his Tim Horton's Timbits? (I add local colour and pathos to their gig, he kindly says.) Yes, I might be congenitally fickle, but I'm no rat. Me. Amicus of Osgoode, Q.C. for Questing Cat. A stool-pigeon? A canary? A Tweetie-Pie?*

Now I can see, anyway, that there is something to the argument that dumping accused people in the dock offends the presumption of innocence. That's why in the United States and Nova Scotia they put them at the table with their lawyers — to avoid the appearance that their guilt is a foregone conclusion. The dock itself is down and out, a poor cousin to all the other fittings provided for the dramatis personae in the proceedings. The room's wainscotting is blonde oak panelling, and the judge sits atop a similarly panelled dais, her clerk and voice stenographer at its base.

Above her is a colourful and impressive crest reading *Dieu et mon droit*. The body of the court is fenced off by a polished oak "bar" and swinging gate, just like the courtrooms you see on television. But the prisoner's dock is constructed, at its base, of utility-grade lumber — plywood, maybe, or fibreboard — in which the indifferent carpenter has set a Plexiglas shield, the whole assembly reaching about as high as the shoulders of an average-size man. Hands and arms and foreheads and even cheeks — mortal desolation — have smudged the Plexiglas beyond recognition. To Canadian eyes, it is reminiscent of nothing so much as the penalty box in ice hockey.

"What's your position on this, Mr. Mortimer?" Justice M'Gonnigle turns to Crown counsel.

Then shalt thou answer them-a, Like as ye have forsaken me, and served strange gods in your land-a, so shall ye serve strangers in a land that is not yours.

Mortimer hefts all 285 pounds of himself to his feet and huffs over his nicotine-stained salt-and-pepper goatee. "Well, in principle we wouldn't object, Your Honour." Reeking of tobacco and pocked with cigarette burns, his gown barely fits, and it certainly does not disguise his heft. His tabs, reddled with tobacco to match his beard and fingers after too many frostbitten fag breaks in the courtyard between 361 and Osgoode Hall, look to choke the poor sod. "But as Your Honour says, we are in mid-trial and I'm right in mid chief, of Mrs. Debeers. The poor old jury's cooling its heels again, and I haven't heard anything that sounds like a persuasive argument that my learned friend should remove himself."

"Don't toady, Snerd," Nobb stage-whispers out of the side of his mouth, loudly enough for the judge and all the rest of us to hear. "Poor old jury my poor old arthritic foot!" I believe the modern term for this particular hockey manoeuvre is "talking trash."

Mortimer studiously ignores him. "I've got witnesses here all ready to go, and they've got family responsibilities, as well as other work to go to, to earn their crust. As does the jury. I mean, justice delayed is justice denied, Your Honour."

Nobb has not bothered to sit during Mortimer's submissions. "If Mr. Snerd, er, Mr. Mortimer will look up from his dictionary of worn-out clichés a moment, Your Honour, he'll see that no one's denying justice to anyone, and I resent the insinuation that I, as an officer of this honourable court, would delay justice to my own client or waste the court's valuable time. Indeed, Your Honour, I'm trying to promote justice here, precisely, to get my client out of a potential conflict situation, which could work to her prejudice, and to mine, as an officer of your court. Your Honour."

The judge sighs and closes her *Criminal Code*. Nobb suddenly relaxes, pursing his lips so as not to be tempted to push his luck. Experience proves itself. He slings his robe bag over his shoulder as Justice M'Gonnigle asks, "Has your client made alternative arrangements, then, Mr. Nobb?"

It's as if poor Katrina, the wicked babushka witch, the star villain of the proceedings — her eyes darting over the dock's stained Plexiglas from judge to counsel and back again — it's as though she isn't even there.

"Yes, we do have other counsel in mind for her, Your Honour." *We do?* "Of course we do. It's all taken care of. And with Mr. Gaunt's help, new counsel can be ready to go by next week. Meanwhile, the Crown can finish with Mrs. Debeers, here, with Mr. Gaunt acting for Ms. Slovenskaya in my absence. I don't see any problem with that, Your Honour. He's a capable man, Mr. Gaunt, top student, clerk to Mr. Justice Mariner of the Court of Appeal."

Acknowledging the compliment as Her Honour grimly takes his measure from on high, Gaunt rises and bows, sneezing loudly onto the counsel table.

"Let's proceed then, Mr. Mortimer." Her Honour nods wearily at Conchita Presenkowski, the court clerk. "Order to go removing Mr. Nobb as counsel of record. Mr. Gaunt, you're in the game, sir."

What, exactly, precipitated this mysterious crisis? In his opening, Mortimer told the jury he would present evidence suggesting that the accused, Katrina Daniella Slovenskaya, committed premeditated murder by electrocution. The evidence was circumstantial, but that didn't make it any less persuasive, ladies and gentlemen (Mortimer smiled and nodded at the jury here), when you weighed it all up together. It led, in fact, to a single conclusion, in the Crown's view, but which the jury still was obliged to weigh fairly against the defence evidence, as Her Honour would explain to them at the end of the trial. "It's the old, familiar story, ladies and gentlemen. The Crown's conclusion is that the lonely, middle-aged spinster, as we used to say, the embittered woman before you in the prisoner's dock, Katrina Slovenskaya, acted out of jealousy and greed."

"You've been reading too many third-rate mystery novels, Gordie," Nobb hissed at Mortimer, who put his hands behind his back and made an obscene, nicotine-stained gesture toward the defence table, a gesture which I am led to believe has to do with birds, or perhaps with their beaks.

"This lonely woman was enamoured of the deceased man, Mr. Debeers," Mortimer continued, "only to discover that he did not feel the same way about her. And the evidence will further suggest that she had enjoyed certain business dealings with him such that her profits stood to increase if Jerry Debeers was out of the picture — if she didn't have to share those profits with him." She therefore stood guilty as charged, the Crown believed, of first-degree murder.

"So I repeat," Mortimer concluded, "it's that same old story, members of the jury." He turned and bowed to Nobb. "Straight out of a third-rate pulp mystery novel: trying to have it all, for love or money."

Nobb made a brief speech about how the Crown had absolutely no hard evidence against Ms. Slovenskaya, well-known as a quiet and gentle assistant law librarian — an adopter, indeed, of homeless cats and dogs — who lived a modest and productive life with her sister in East York. Nor indeed would the Crown produce anything beyond grandiose speculation about romantic or business entanglements between his client — a person who had reason to know about the rule of law and the consequences of crime — and his (Nobb's) late, lamented colleague, bencher Jerry Debeers. As Her Honour would explain to them in detail, they could convict only if they had absolutely no reasonable doubt as to his client's guilt. In this case, there was more than a reasonable doubt; there were overwhelming doubts, uncertainties, and questions every which way you turned — nothing like solid proof. While the circumstances of Mr. Debeers' death were unusual and tragic, there was certainly nothing to show that Ms. Slovenskaya had the inclination or ability to arrange it in the bizarre way it had occurred. "This bookish woman of a certain age sitting in the dock here before you, ladies and gentleman, I urge you to take a good, hard look at her."

We all did as Nobb suggested, turning toward the accused, kitted out in the dock in the old-lady's cotton print dress and faded cardigan that Nobb had chosen for her from the wardrobe Katrina's younger sister, Nadia, had brought into his office. Her hair done up in a granny's slightly unkempt bun, Katrina stared bravely ahead, blinking, her face and round little nose reddening with the attention.

"I hope you'll excuse my reference to Ms. Slovenskaya's age and demeanour. But it's important, I suggest, and calls on your everyday experience as reasonable and worldly people. I ask you. Is that not the very picture of your local librarian you see before you? Or is she, members of the jury, your by-the-hour, double-time-on-weekends, blue jeans falling down his bum electrical contractor, no cheques please and travel time's extra?"

Well done, Nobby, I had whispered, some of my doubts about the old toff easing up. *The woman couldn't fork a stuck bagel out of her own toaster without setting her kitchen on fire.*

Then Mortimer called his first witness, the crime-scene pathologist. Using police photos from the Journals Room, the pathologist described the location of Debeers' death and its manner: cardiac arrest, precipitated by electrocution. He added that a younger man, or someone with an altogether healthy heart, might have survived the shock, but that was mere speculation. It was clear, anyway, that Debeers would not have died but for the electrical shock. Nobb chose not to cross-examine, and just before his sudden application to be removed from the case, the Crown was examining Jerry Debeers' mother as its own witness.

"Now Mrs. Debeers," Mortimer was saying, some minutes into his examination, "I know this is difficult for you and I apologize. But can you tell the jury if your son had any other women in his life besides your good self?"

"Well, zere vuz a girl he liked at zuh library zere, he vuz telling me zo."

"And is that girl, that woman, in the courtroom today?"

Anika Debeers squinted her cloudy old eyes and made a brief survey of the room, turning for the sake of completeness to have a good shufty at Justice M'Gonnigle, whose own eyes widened in astonishment behind her spectacles. "Nope. Not so's you'd notice it. Nope."

"It wasn't the accused in the prisoner's dock?"

"Slovenskaya?" Mrs. Debeers laughed, the wrinkles growing positively cavernous around her mouth and eyes. "You gotta be joking, mister. The woman I'm talking about, she liked him, like zuh convict Slovenskaya liked him, too. Ja. He vuz a popular guy wiz the ladies, my Jerry. Is a hard sing to find a decent Christian man zese days, you know, sir. But zis was another one zat worked zere in zuh library. And she wasn't available at zuh moment, if you see vut I'm saying. You know, for the dating scene, like. She vuz married, this vun. And she has zuh two kids, already. And zo I used to be telling my Jerry you should get over it, she's not zuh vun for you, zis vun. And anyvays, he says he has to look after his old mum, ya know, and ve vuz doing fine, us. When I vent, he was gonna have ever's'ing, him and his brudder, Mr. Crown. Ve vuz doing fine, zere, on our own, sir."

"But you know Katrina Slovenskaya?"

"Mostly by name, ja. She was my son's friend. And me and Slovenskaya is directors of my son's company. Ja."

Nobb shot to his feet. "Your Honour, the Crown has disclosed absolutely nothing to us indicating that the deceased Mr. Debeers was involved in any company with my client."

Justice M'Gonnigle looked inquisitively at Mortimer.

"I'm getting there, Your Honour," he said, moderately apologetic.

"Not if I have anything to do with it," Nobb cut in. "We haven't seen anything to this effect, and if he goes on like this, I'm going to move for a stay of proceedings given the Crown's failure to make full and fair disclosure."

"Your Honour, if I could just proceed, Mr. Nobb will see that he has everything that we have, and there's no use snapping his suspenders at me like this and getting all in a flap."

"Flapping's my thing, Mortimer," Nobb responded. "Not to mention my duty. And you, in turn, sir, have the absolute duty to permit us to make full answer and defence. To disclose all your evidence to us."

"You'll proceed very deliberately, Mr. Mortimer," the judge warned the Crown, while glaring at Nobb. "And Mrs. Debeers, you will pause before answering to see if I have anything to say first. Is that clear?"

"Yes, Your Majesty," Anika Debeers said. Then she stood briefly and bowed to the bench.

"I am showing the witness a piece of paper, Your Honour, and I will be asking that it be marked as an exhibit," Mortimer continued.

"Can I see that first?" Nobb asked. Examining the sheet, he turned quite pale, then the russet red of a fall beet, clashing only a little with his sanguinary robing bag. "I guess I'm bringing that motion right now, Your Honour, if you could excuse the jury."

Mortimer actually buzzed his lips. "Number one, he can't, Your Honour, because he hasn't given notice to the provincial and federal attorneys general. Number two, in the circumstances, he can't possibly say he's taken by surprise."

Justice M'Gonnigle examined the piece of paper. "I'm going to let you proceed, Mr. Mortimer, but slowly, because I might still be inclined to give Mr. Nobb an adjournment to bring his constitutional motion about disclosure. We'll see. Members of the jury, please just concentrate on the evidence from the witness, not on what we're saying here about so-called disclosure. It's a technical matter in constitutional law, and it's not for you to worry about. Please just concentrate on the facts of the case. On what actually happened, not on the legal jargon."

"Mrs. Debeers." Mortimer turned back to his witness. "Do you recognize this piece of paper?"

"I never seen it before, but it's my son's handwriting, I can say zat to you for sure, sir. Ja."

"Thank you. Now, can you tell us, did you hold shares in that company you just mentioned?"

"Ja. I got seven shares."

"You're an investor?"

"Ja. I'm an investor. Small time. I got seven. The convict, she's got three."

"You mean the accused?"

"Yeah, her, three shares. And Jerry, he's got fifteen, for the time being."

"And what sort of company was it?"

"Real estate investment velcro, he's telling me, my Jerry."

"Vehicle? Real estate investment *vehicle*?"

"Ja, real estate velcro. Institutional, like. You know, nursing home, old folks home, or something. Commercial. With food services and housekeeping and whadayoucall. Lots of different opportunities, is why we liked it. Lots room for the growth, for spread the risk, that sort of stuff, you know? I don't know. Somesing. One thing don't work, plan B works, you know? Diversified, they call it."

"Now if you look at the paper again . . ."

Nobb began to rise, but the judge warned him off: "No flapping and snapping, please, Mr. Nobb."

"If you look at the paper again, please, Mrs. Debeers," Mortimer continued, "Do you see where it says 'Debeers' with a diagonal line, and then it says "A 7."

Ah, that paper. The paper Inspector Yastremski showed Fitz-Niblick, with the names and the numbers.

"Ja. Dot's me. A. Debeers, seven shares. Because see there's a fifteen next to Debeers, J, zere, see dot? Dot's my Jerry. And next to the question mark, it's a three, which it's Slovenskaya."

"Where it says 'E.T.' and then a question mark?"

"Ja, Slovenskaya, see, we put her in zere, and next . . ."

"Your Honour, I really must insist," Nobb was on his feet and sweating into the creases at his cheeks.

"Mr. Mortimer," Justice M'Gonnigle responded. "Can we perhaps move past what's exactly on the paper, then? I think we have the point of it, and Mr. Nobb is having kittens. We see that apparently it's a list of shareholders in this company. I mean, technically, it's hearsay, I guess, at this point, anyway. I guess we need to know what it has to do with the price of beans here, if you get my drift, Mr. Mortimer."

"Yes, ma'am. And to that end I want to ask a little more about the deceased's interest in the company. I don't think that's clear enough yet."

"Stick to that, please, then. And ask her only what she can tell us from her personal knowledge."

"Thank you, Your Honour. Mrs. Debeers, so you and Jerry were both investors?"

"Yeah. He's telling me I'm gonna get a lot more out of it than just the next-to-smallest shareholder. He's telling me he's fixing it up things so's we can buy out the major shareholders."

"Mr. Mortimer, I can see that Mr. Nobb is getting nervous about her putting words in her son's mouth. And so am I."

"Yes, Your Honour, but of course poor Mr. Debeers is not here to assist us, and I'm not going much farther with this."

"I would think not. Unless you want to apply to go farther. We'll need to excuse the jury."

"It won't be necessary, Your Honour. I can move on. Mrs. Debeers, when you say 'we' could buy out the other shareholders, what do you, yourself, mean by that?"

"I mean me and Jerry. And Slovenskaya, maybe. Mostly me and Jerry. Slovenskaya at first, because we need her. First, we think maybe that other girl, the library girl, but we decide Slovenskaya. She likes my Jerry. Jerry's making nice with her because we're needing her as friend. Just zuh business friend, see, for zuh three shares. And then we buy her, too. Then, goodbye Slovenskaya, and good riddance."

"And did Jerry do that — fix things so you and he could buy more shares?"

"Not yet, sir. There was complicating factors, he says. Things was getting a little tricky and I start I'm worrying about my investor money, you know, and it was real complicated. I'm an old age pension, you know, Mr. Mortencrown, and I put my Jerry through his law school and to become a lawyer like this, and I don't have the money to just throw it around the place. And Jerry, he's put up all his own money he had into the businesses, every dime from his practice, Your Crownship, and he mortgaged my house, which was now his house, too, see, joint tenants, like our chequing account, and he used up even our little line of credit at the bank, there, too, and they was giving him a hard time about it, I'll telling you, all so he could get moneys for the companies, the investment, see. So, finally, we have a fight, Jerry and me. A argument, you know, not a fight, I'm exaggerate, Jerry says, all the times, a argument, I mean, not so really a bad one, you know." Here, the witness sniffled, but proved adamant about getting the story out. "A discussion, you know?, and I tell him I vant my money back." The old woman struck the edge of the witness box, as though her poor, errant son were before her at the very moment, pleading that her money was all tied up. "This is no safe investment, no safe for me, I says, and he says if I could just be wait and act patient that damn journalist was snooping around the place, and so was Probert, besides, sir."

"And Probert was who?"

"Probert. That Josey Probert. You know, another one she's a big cheese people at the Law Society, where my Jerry was on the board or whaddaya call 'im. She was another one, she had the eyes for my Jerry, too, you know?"

"His colleague as a bencher?"

"Ja, she vuz sitting like Jerry on the Law Society benches, ja.

They vuz working together a lots of the times. And she likes him, and maybe his investments, I don't know. They vuz going eggspose how some of the other benches was pulling the wools on the other lawyers."

"Expose?" the judge asked.

"Yes, Your Majesty, eggspose. The members, you know, that they was boss of, like, eggspose them the dirty business, the other benches was cheating on them, all the lawyers. The bosses, the big cheeses benches at the Law Society, they was drinking up the vines and all that for themselves."

"The wines?"

"You got it, judge, but not my Jerry," Mrs. Debeers shakes her head at Justice M'Gonnigle. "Jerry he's not no drinker. Some of the other ones there, the big shots from the Bay Street. And Josey and Jerry was beating them out of the bushes, you know, like when you hunt your foods, only this was vines, too, to make them face the music, like, out of the bushes."

And it was then, amid these colourfully mixed metaphors and motivations, that Nobb finally succeeded in removing himself from the record. In the ensuing hubbub he gathers up his spectacle case, his pens, his yellow sticky-notes, his binder, then he turns as if he wants to say something important to Leland Gaunt sitting expectantly behind him. Nobb hesitates, frowns at the table, then silently high-tails it out of the courtroom, his silk robe billowing in his jet-stream, the *Criminal Code* in his monogrammed, blood-red robe-bag bump-thumping against his flank.

CHAPTER 2

Demonstrative Evidence

Leland Gaunt's pale green herringbone sports jacket hangs loosely on his meagre frame, not so much because it is too large but because he seems to be trying to shrink within its fabric to hide, or maybe to doze in its inner pocket. Colourwise, it does not really work with his dark brown twill trousers. Nor does his skinny little pink tie match any other clothing he wears, dotted though it is with greenish-yellow French horns. As the court waits expectantly, Gaunt stands at his place two rows back from the court's well, still in his junior's spot behind where Nobb lately begged off. Gaunt snuffles, rubs at his nose with a knuckle, shifts on his scuffed Hush Puppies, clears his throat, then looks at the ceiling, craning and exercising his neck. Someone coughs. The jurors look at their hands. "Your Honour," Gaunt begins at last, "I'd like to show the witness Exhibit 3A." His words seem to come directly from his nose, in a sort of combination bark and honk, as though he were a performing goose.

The witness is shown a piece of paper. Another eternity passes and several new universes are born.

"Mrs. Debeers, can you tell the jury the nature of the document I'm showing you?"

"Nature?" The witness looks wide-eyed at the judge for help.

"What does it say on top?" the judge assists.

"Ontario Ministry of Consumer and Commercial Relations?"

"Yes," the judge says, "and the line after that?"

"Says Form 1, Ontario Corporation, Initial Return, Notice of Change."

"And at the bottom?" Gaunt says.

"Is my name. Anika Debeers."

"Your name in what context?"

Before Mrs. Debeers can look up at Justice M'Gonnigle and ask "What context?" the judge says, "Yes, yes, Mr. Gaunt, we've already established that this is the corporation Mr. Debeers set up and that the witness is a director, along with Ms. Slovenskaya. You're a director of this corporation, isn't that right, Mrs. Debeers?"

"A director. Ja. Really I'm investor only, judge. Director just for say-so. Ja."

Gaunt blinks and looks as if he's about to weep. He rubs his nose again, then honks: "Okay, then. Well, what about the line numbered seven there? Do you see that?"

"Ja," the witness responds. "Seven."

"And there's a row of boxes there, labelled alphabetically, A to R."

"Little boxes, ja."

"Can you tell us which box has an 'x' in it."

"Ja, dot's easy. Box number Q."

"Okay, now turn over the page please."

"Ja. Over."

"You see in the middle where it says 'Code, Type of Business'?"

"Ja, code. Ja."

"What does it say after 'Q'?"

"Says 'Accommodation, Food, Beverage Service Industries.'"

"So that would be the type of business your corporation does? Accommodation, food, beverage, service industries?"

"No. No food beverage. We was in real estate developments. The other one, that vun, ve had it already, it vuz the food beverage. Not this vun, real estate."

Gaunt blinks and rubs his nose again. "'Kay, then," he says. "Turn the paper back over."

"Ja."

"Look at those codes again, please. Can you find the one that says 'Real Estate Operator'?"

We all hold our breath without really noticing until Anika Debeers at last answers, "Ja, Real Operator. Dot's number L. Operator. Real estate."

"'Kay. Now turn the paper back over."

"Ja."

"There's no mark in the L box, is there?"

"Nope. No L. You got zat right, Mr. Accuse."

Satisfied with this devastating cross-examination, Gaunt slumps back into his seat and sneezes.

Please do not allow your dog to urinate on the lawnmowers next door.

Ruminating over this notice has cheered me considerably after what I have been through this afternoon. Contemplating its subtext as I doze in the cut-down Humpty Dumpty potato chip carton in my corner of the Reference Room at the Great Library, deconstructing the sign's syntax and plurisignative ambiguities, have gone some distance to restoring my dislocated dignity.

Please do not allow your dog to urinate on the lawnmowers next door.

According to law professor H.L.A. Hart, a law is a rule with a sanction. The urinating on lawnmowers sign is a not-law, because, even if you could call it a rule, there is no necessary or defined punishment for defying it. If you pee on the lawnmowers, there is no necessary consequence. But as Justice Mariner likes to tell law students and anyone else who will listen, such not-laws are the mortar, the "grey area," that binds civil society. They are the social contract whereby we do the right thing not because we have to, but because it is the right thing. Wise guys and the terminally selfish, as we are about to learn in Madam Justice Hosanna M'Gonnigle's court on University Avenue, live on the fringes of these grey areas. They scrape away at the not-law mortar between the law bricks until all the bricks come tumbling down on top of them, and on us. And civilization crumbles.

Law is law, but not-law can be justice.

Anyway, I think that the not-law *Please do not allow your dog to urinate on the lawnmowers next door* (I just seem to love repeating that today, again and again, dreamily, musingly) has become my favourite sign in the known universe. Maybe it is only the drugs talking, but this placard seems to have displaced my previous favourite sign in the galaxy, if not the universe: *This space reserved for the Master of the Universe*. That one used to stand sentry over a parking space at the Divine Light Mission near Spadina and College. And I always thought that it took unbelievable generosity of spirit to put your faith in a master of the universe who needed a reservation.

True, it seems you need a reservation everywhere these days. His Lordship doesn't eat in the Barrister's Dining Room any more, as I say, although it's right here at the Hall and is widely noted for its cuisine. He can't just go in any more and have his meal when he can squeeze it into his day — never mind his loyal custom for more than two decades. It's become chi-chi, the public place to be, and you won't be served unless you've reserved your spot days in advance, justice of appeal or not. And that just doesn't work, does it, when you're sitting in court and you never know exactly what the day will bring?

Still, even in the so-called, once-was Barrister's Dining Room, would any self-respecting master of the universe need a reservation?

But groggily I digress. Yes, maybe it's the drugs that make me smile over this newer sign, the drugs they gave me to make me sleep (fancy, having to give a cat drugs to make him sleep!), so that they could clean my teeth at the Eglinton Veterinary Hospital, where His Lordship had sent me with his secretary, the primly efficient Ms. Sandy Pargeter, this afternoon. "He smells like a garbage strike at the fish market," His Lordship had complained. Actually, it was quite literally eau de toilette, because that's what was available to slake my thirst at the time, but it was certainly designer eau de toilette, straight from the shining if dribble-dottled porcelain in the justices' washroom. And was it my fault that His Lordship had fallen asleep on the couch in his chambers, and then suddenly awakened, snuffling and snorting and all discombobulated, late for something terribly important, to find me napping companionably on his chest?

His own breath wasn't exactly cherry blossoms on the

Hokkaido River. If he hadn't yawned, himself, the contagion to do the same in reply wouldn't have been in the air, and then I wouldn't have opened my own yap right under his nose, just before I licked him affectionately right on his plump little judicial lips to ask: *Pleasant dreams, Sleeping Beauty?* Lick. Lick.

Doesn't he occasionally speak with similar affection to Yours Groggily? I mean, I thought the feeling was beginning to be mutual. More fool I.

Rise and shine, I added, lick, lick, affectionately mimicking what he always says to me, albeit usually while nudging me with his fat toe. *There's justice to be done.* Lick. Lick.

And it must be seen to be done, I always reply, in the best traditions of the Bar. As a cat learned in the law, I can spout legal maxims with the best of 'em. But today there is no justice apparent.

"Aiiee!" cries he, dragging his sleeve across his now dewy lips, spitting and thrusting out his tongue most rudely against my kisses, shooting to his feet, so that I fly straight onto the nearest bookshelf, carom off His Lordship's *Tremeaar's Criminal Pleadings*, then plummet straight-legged and wide-eyed to the floor, which I touch only at a skitter, on the desperate tips of my fully arched claws, until I am right out the door — which fortunately is slightly ajar.

But my escape is short-lived. A new term is solemnly added to my probation order: It's off forthwith to the Eglinton Veterinary Hospital — where His Lordship always takes his idiot mutt, Stong — for a complete checkup, flea bath, ear mite treatment, and, far worst of all, general anaesthesia followed by an hour's scaling of the old dentition at the tender mercies of the veterinary dental hygienist.

Of course, on the way into the vet's, through the wire mesh on the front of my carrier, I see the hardware store one door west. And as it is a fine late summer's day, there are barbecue units on display on the front walkway, along with garden tools, a picnic table, a wheelbarrow, and yes, various grass-cutting machines. Yes, maybe it's the drugs. On the way out, I have to smile. Beatifically. Blissed out. De-fleaed, de-mited, and de-livered from imminent gingivitis. Ms. Pargeter sets me in my carrier on the counter, so that she can pay the bill (out of His Lordship's wallet, it is only fair to add). And that is when I see it, on the wall, near the door, at about eye-level if you're, say, five-foot-one. And that is when I feel even more smug than usual in the quintessence of my catitude, my dignity restored as *felis sylvestris*.

Please do not allow your dog to urinate on the lawnmowers next door.

Now *that*, sir, is justice.

The Crown calls Elise Throckmorton. Pale, slender, beautiful in her consumptive, pre-Raphaelite sort of way — like Millais' Ophelia, an accidental junkie, someone both too lovely and too lonely for this world — she gives her evidence sombrely, her hands clasped before her, her pallid, freckled forearms bare to the elbow in her diaphanous cotton dress. Yes, she had lunch a few times with Jerry Debeers. Yes, he always made a point of chit-chatting with her when he was in the library. Yes, he seemed to like her, yes, even quite a lot. But, no, there was nothing more than that between them. She was stolidly married and had two children of grade-school age. Mind you, Elise does not seem convinced that family life is necessarily an argument against hanky-panky, at least not from my Questing Cat's shin's-eye view of body language. She seems ambivalent, no matter how firmly she says yes or no. Among Has-beings who live in the real world, such is the nature of holy deadlock, I have observed: the putatively happy couple is stuck together with the mortar of compromise and cliché, no matter what nature is trying to tell them. That's civilization, I suppose. Law versus not-Law.

But as Mortimer is about to move on, Elise takes a deep breath and adds: "Besides, he was always trying to convert me. Or get me to be born again, I guess. A believer. He had made me a sort of project."

"Yes," Mortimer says, sorting through his papers and clearly hoping that this is the end of that particular digression. But then he looks up, smiles, and takes a beat, as though something has occurred to him. Lawyers are not supposed to ask a question if they don't already know the answer, but I'm pretty sure Mortimer breaks this rule when he queries, "And did you talk about this with Katrina Slovenskaya — how he seemed to be making a project of you?"

"We laughed about it. Katrina told me to tell him I was Jewish. But I don't think she found it very funny, really. She was sort of protective of Jerry, kind of proprietary. We all were, sometimes, because he had this sort of innocence about him, for all his fervour. A crazed, lit-up sort of innocence, I guess. Evangelistic. Anyway, partly because of that, I didn't want to offend him, so I told him I was a superstitious atheist," Elise goes sadly, ambivalently on, her eyelids aflutter.

"Oh, yes," Mortimer faintly says, looking seasick.

"I read that once in university, in a Robert Browning poem. It just suddenly seemed appropriate, so much more descriptive than, I don't know, 'agnostic,' I guess — and a way out from Jerry's attempts to evangelize. So I just said it. And the more I thought about it, the truer it seemed. I want to believe, you see, but working in the justice system doesn't give you a very positive view of the world, does it?"

"Well, I wouldn't. . . ."

"It makes you cynical, if you see what I mean. Jerry used to say that his mission was to bridge the gap between law and justice. I mean, if there were divine justice, never mind human justice, if there were *any* justice, a man like that, a man like Jerry Debeers, he would still be alive, wouldn't he?"

"One would hope so, certainly," Mortimer replies, looking as though he suddenly feels much better, "and that is why we are trying to do justice here, Ms. Throckmorton. And that is why I, personally, am certainly *not* cynical about the justice system. Nor, I trust, is Her Honour."

"You're toadying again, Snerd," Gaunt hisses.

Then, banally (for if evil is truly banal, justice must endeavour to be the same), Mortimer asks Elise about the photocopier. No, she says, as far as she had known, there was nothing wrong with the photocopier in the Journals Room of the library.

"Cross-examination, Mr. Gaunt?" The judge looks over the top of her Cro-Magnon spectacles at Justice Mariner's clerk, and it strikes me that he and the witness are of a kind, a matching set — your garden-variety brittle, freckle-faced Anglo-Saxon Has-being, deceptively sickly specimens whose forebears somehow made it across the oceans, starving and puking their bellies raw in the fetid, borborygmic bellies of creaking four-masted freighters, Europe's runts fleeing their motherlands to colonize all five continents. The two of them look as if they would break if you clinked them together. And they have a lonely terror in their eyes as though they fear it themselves. Perhaps this is their strength and strategy for survival, their *modus vivendi*: fear as a weapon. So it's probably just as well that Gaunt plays gentle Sir Lancelot to the lissom Lady Guinevere in the box. He asks her one velvet-gloved question, looking at the floor the while:

"Then again, the photocopiers aren't your responsibility, Ms. Throckmorton, are they? Or my client's responsibility, come to that?"

"No. The reading room people look after them. One of the assistants, that's his dedicated job. Everett. Everett Wickham."

Of course, the Crown then calls Everett Wickham, who testifies he wasn't aware of any problem with the photocopier, either, and who faces a suddenly transformed Leland Gaunt. In a withering, merciless cross-examination, the po'-faced law clerk seeks to know exactly how lackadaisically Everett Wickham performs his miserable, dirty, thankless job, and at minimum wage, too, such that the photocopiers limp along without paper, toner, or proper electrical connections for hours, days, on end.

"I have only two hands sir." Wickham shrugs, glaring venomously at Gaunt for the defence.

"Is that why you keep that welcoming little sign on your desk, Mr. Wickham? The little sign that I personally have seen so many times when I need assistance in the library. The sign that says, 'Your lack of planning is not my emergency'?"

In fact, His Lordship and Katrina are sufficiently impressed with Leland-Launcelot Gaunt's conduct of the defence that they have decided he can joust with Mortimer on his own, at least for now. The expense and trouble of briefing senior counsel seems unnecessary. "After Nobb's attempts at being slick," Justice Mariner has told our Katrina during a recess, when the heretofore feckless Gaunt is out of earshot (earnestly sketching out his merciless cross-examinations in his office, no doubt), "Leland's gawkiness is our new asset, I would say. He looks like the sort of lawyer that suits us as an honest, unassuming, wrongly accused librarian. He's honest, unassuming, wrongly accused, himself." His Lordship laughed. "Bookish, ingenuous, even — honest to a fault. Let's keep him for the time being, eh? Leland Gaunt, Nebbish for the Defence. A little sad. A little lonely. A little like everybody else in this sordid little melodrama."

A little sad. A little lonely. A little like everybody else in this sordid little melodrama. Years ago, in one of those Kensington Market alleyways infused with rotting produce and the metallic bouquet of fish oil, I came across the front section from the *Globe and Mail*, momentarily underfoot or perhaps stuck to the ground in that pungent, back alley muck — which for all we know could contain the secrets of the origins of life. An article caught my eye, a little feature just under the front-page fold, about "the changing face of Canada," if I remember correctly, the "emerging multiculturalism." What I recall quite clearly, anyway, is that the reporter interviewed a new arrival to Toronto, an immigrant from Russia, smiling wanly in the accompanying photo. Of his new home this fellow gypsy said something I shall never forget: "You are like your Canadian sun: shining but not warm."

This is my experience here, too, of course. Justice Mariner likes to say "we've all become items on our friends' To Do lists." I come to see that I am worn out by the world's indifference whenever an act of kindness surprises me almost to tears, like the sudden warmth of the springtime sun emerging from the clouds. But being somewhat more self-reliant, or perhaps simply more cynical, than humans, the cat instinctively defeats incipient loneliness with distraction, even if it's nothing more than a mote of dust or the scent of rain in a gust of wind. The world is so full of curiosities and diversions, it would seem pointless to expend much time on sadness — which, after all, is nothing more than another fact of life. Yes, melancholy has its profound uses: it renders us capable of deeper thought and feeling. But there is goodness in the world, kindness, compassion, beauty, sometimes produced out of melancholy itself, which, because it is recreative, is not the same thing as despair. The trick is not to forget this. The trick is to concentrate on small miracles, from orange blossoms and seahorses to the serpent's tooth and the tiger's stripes, animal, vegetable, and mineral wantonly shucking and jiving together in Creation's photosynthetic Light and Music Show. *Glory be to God for dappled things.* But yes, of course Mortimer has a point. For all the clamour, the posturing, the rushing hugger-mugger hither and yon, the self-righteous argument echoing through its palatial meeting rooms and dining halls and libraries, back and forth in its courtrooms and chambers, up and down its grand staircases and in its grey drywall-and-linoleum back rooms, offices, and toilets, the Hall is a monument to human desolation, an architectural Cinderella, the belle of the ball, hiding her desolate, aching breast under her renovated gown as her heart's blood sings, *You're born alone. You live alone. You die alone.* In its garish, faded beauty it is a museum of life's misery. Just ask Jeremiah Debeers.

Or Shirley Duguay of Richmond, Prince Edward Island. For three days in early October, 1994, Shirley's five children waited in vain for her to come home. The tiny (eighty-five-pound) homemaker was on welfare, it seems, so she did not have many regular appointments or obligations. Then, on October 7, someone found Shirley's car in the woods near Tyne Valley, a few miles away. Technicians with the Royal Canadian Mounted Police discovered traces of Shirley's blood on the seats, as well as on a T-shirt and a pillow the police found about half a mile away. In early November, the Mounties came upon a man's bloodstained leather jacket wrapped in a plastic bag and hidden in the woods about four miles from Shirley's home. The blood was Shirley Duguay's.

Another six months later, a fisherman found Shirley's rotting corpse in a shallow grave in the woods of North Enmore, about nine miles from where police located the car. She had been viciously beaten about the face and head, and her hands were tethered behind her back.

The police suspected that Shirley's estranged common-law husband, thirty-five-year-old Doug Beamish, had killed her. About ten years earlier, when Beamish's first common-law wife had turned down his inebriated demands for sex, he had punched her in the face, raped her, and held a butcher knife to her throat, warning her in front of her sobbing young children that he intended to kill her. Later the same day, Beamish went for a bath and pulled the woman's head down to him in the tub by her hair, advising her, sincerely and truthfully, that as he had cut the telephone wires, she was powerless against him.

As part of their investigation into the Duguay murder, the P.E.I. police collected several white cat hairs from the bloody jacket's lining. They sent the hairs to the Laboratory of Genomic Diversity at the National Cancer Institute in Frederick, Maryland, which recently had set up a databank of cat DNA. The lab had the Mounties collect blood from Snowball, a short-haired cat owned by Doug Beamish's parents, and from nineteen sundry cats in P.E.I. Using this data, and samples from nine other cats in the United States, the lab was able to show with about ninety-five per cent certainty that the hairs in the jacket had belonged to Snowball. Like Snowball, Beamish lived with his parents. And he had been seen wearing the jacket, or at least one like it, the day before Duguay disappeared. Armed with that evidence, on July 19, 1996, a jury convicted Beamish of the second-degree murder of Shirley Duguay.

As the Crown's next witness in *The Queen v. Slovenskaya* explains in his faded Scottish brogue, the scientists at the Genomic Diversity lab briefly discuss their work on the Beamish case in the journal *Nature* for April 24, 1997, page 774. The witness, Austin Rowse, is himself a forensic DNA expert at the Centre for Forensic Sciences in Toronto. To begin his Powerpoint presentation to the jury, he projects a copy of the *Nature* article onto a screen set up next to him in the witness box. Then he shows the court a chart he has prepared, a chart very like the one in the *Nature* article, which compares the Snowball data to the hairs found on Doug Beamish's jacket.

At the top of the first two columns on Rowse's chart we can all read the names of Katrina Slovenskaya's cats, Grimalkin in column one, Mingus in column two. Above column four, the heading says, "Foil Evidence." Atop column three, between the columns labelled Mingus and Foil Evidence, Rowse has typed, Amicus (Osgoode Lib. Cat). And here I'd thought it was the annual rabies vaccine malarkey when they had come at me with that syringe:

Grimalkin	Mingus	Amicus (Osgoode Lib. Cat)	Foil	Evidence

"Could you tell the court where the aluminum foil came from?" Mortimer asks Rowse.

"The police collected it at the scene of Mr. Debeers' death. As you can see in the police photographs, it was wrapped around the cord on the photocopier. Just below the plug."

"Yes, the jury has heard evidence about that. And can you tell them what your studies of the foil revealed?"

"Well, it was burnt, apparently from the electrical current running through it, but we were able to recover some hairs, as well as some residue from what turned out to be food. The hairs and food were mixed."

"Tell us about the hairs, Dr. Rowse. What sorts of hairs?"

"They were the cat hairs I've mentioned."

"How did you determine that?"

"From the DNA. The genes that make up the hairs."

"And you could tell that even though they were mixed in with the food?"

"Oh, yes. I mean, from microscopic and DNA points of view, it's all quite distinct. One doesn't affect the other much."

"And of what use were the hairs to your analysis of the foil?"

"Well, once we determined what we had, we obtained a search

warrant, and we were able to take hair and blood samples from the accused woman's cats, and compare them to the hairs on the foil."

"Which cats do you mean?"

"Well, you can see on the chart that they are Grimalkin, an eleven-year-old female mix, and Mingus, an eight-year-old tom. Ms. Slovenskaya's pet cats, at her home."

"But you were explaining that you need a larger sample for accuracy's sake?"

"Yes. For that, and for purposes of elimination, we collected samples from a cat in residence at Osgoode Hall — at least it's here temporarily, I understand." The witness chuckles. "A busy-body stray, I'm told, that the staff has taken in. That's the one up there in the fourth column, called Amicus. With the help of the zoology department at the University of Toronto, we were also able to collect samples from about six strays that live in the vicinity of Osgoode Hall, and from various cats in the university laboratories and veterinary facilities. To fill out the sample and make it more accurate. You know, more encompassing."

"And this food residue. Would that affect the accuracy of identifying which cat belonged to which hair?"

"No, in fact it helped us identify where the foil came from and sort of tie everything in together. It has fat from cheese and sausage on it, and as I say, that doesn't affect the DNA code in the hairs."

"And the burning didn't affect the hairs or anything on there?"

"Well, not everything was burnt. You see, the moisture made the foil even more conductive of electricity. Which means it would have passed that more easily into Mr. Debeers' hand without heating up the foil quite as much."

"And what did the hair samples tell you?"

"With about ninety-seven per cent accuracy, we can say that the hairs came from the three cats on the chart."

"Katrina Slovenskaya's cats?"

"Well, her cats, and the one who would have been snooping around the library and maybe nosing around in her lunch, I understand. Amicus there, the library cat."

I decide that this might be a good time to go outside for a pee.

"Just stick to what you know, Dr. Rowse," I hear Justice M'Gonnigle warn. Glancing up at the bench as I depart, I see Her Honour widen her eyes librarian-like and consider the scientist witness over the black rim of those Cro-Magnon eyebrow specs.

I can't make my escape soon enough. As I wait for someone to use the door so I can slip through, Mortimer calls the detectives who worked on the Jeremiah Debeers case, and Sergeant Donovan testifies about stumbling upon the electrical toolkit in Katrina Slovenskaya's desk — the one with the strippers, wirecutters, electrical tape, and greasy foil. Then, as court adjourns for the day, the Crown informs Justice M'Gonnigle that its last witness is to be Josey Probert.

You're born alone, you live alone, you die alone. Just ask Ernie the Evangelist. With baling twine, he has hung a sign on the Hall's black iron fence where it faces the streetcar shelter on Queen Street and the Sheraton Hotel across the street. It flaps about against the fence, stigmatic against the grey streets and rainy skies.

In marker-pen on the back of a cardboard panel from a case of Crown Royal whisky he has scrawled:

For I have heard a voice as of a woman in travail, and the anguish as of her that bringeth forth her first child, the voice of the daughter of Zion, that bewaileth herself, that spreadeth her hands, saying, Woe is me now! For my soul is wearied because of murderers.
Jeremiah IV, 31

CHAPTER 3

Bargain Basement Justice

Despite the manifold distractions of the Squirrel Wars, we have reached page 37 in "Environmentalist Protesters and the *Public Lands Act:* Reasonable Limits on the 'Reasonable Limits' We Impose on Free Expression and Mobility Rights," which is now a mere 167 days late. It would appear, however, that the enemy has infiltrated our front lines. That, anyway, is what I deduce from the shift in our thesis. Nearly a year ago, Justice Mariner had set out to argue that the state's attempts to restrain free expression by protesters was presumptively wrong — wrong, that is, unless the authorities could demonstrate immediate danger of public disorder and the spread of violence. When a tree-hugger goes wrong. . . . "Beyond the civil liberties considerations," His Lordship had written (but now has scribbled through while backhanding me to one side off his papers),

> *preservation of the environmental resources is oftentimes a superior goal to the short-term profit of immediate harvest of timber or diversion of natural waterways. Conservation in this sense is not "tree-hugging," but prudent resource*

*management and a reasonable expression of political econ-
omy. It would be odd, indeed, if we employed trespass law
as a blunt instrument against those taking action in favour
of the long-term economic as well as environmental benefits
of such regulation. Even when showing off in blue jeans and
headbands, even at its most youthfully exuberant and narcissistic, protest can work to the general societal good.*

It seemed reasonable enough to Yours Editorially. Now, though, it appears that we have gone over to that far Caesarian shore: Laws which limit tree-hugger protests constitute a reasonable limit on free expression — "such reasonable limits as are demonstrably justified in a free and democratic society," as our *Charter of Rights and Freedoms* puts it. Economically, and at this point of deep recession in the world economies, environmental activists have yelled fire in a crowded national forest. At the end of the day their right of expression is less important than the more general public good of free commerce, unrestrained trade of commodities, development of dependable world economies, the usual globalization folderol. In other words, If God had wanted us to save the trees he wouldn't have given us chainsaws. It is beyond Your Exasperated Reporter why His Lordship doesn't simply scrawl that across the whole works and be done with it, in 32-point type.

In manifest disgust, I move to the window. I mewl a little, growl softly, do the time-lapse pansy-blooming thing with my irises, chatter the old incisors, even hiss a bit, until at last I get His Lordship's full attention. He comes to see what I see. And yes, while I was hoping to distract him from his hopelessly reactionary tirade about saving the Carolinian forests or old-growth maples from all the ageing granolas singing "We Shall Overcome," I must admit to having a deeper ulterior motive. I remain in mercy, myself, after all: I still have to prove my own long-term worth as a local natural resource lest the old salt gets permanently fed up with me and sends me off to gaol, a.k.a. Her Majesty's Dog House and Inhumane Society — chops me down in full flower, as it were. So now we share the view, companion human and faithful feline consultant, down into the front courtyard, where a few lonely apricots hang on the farthest reaches of the trees' remotest branches. It is like the last days of the dinosaurs. In two seasons we have not salvaged a single ripened fruit, and even now, only eight or ten show the burnish of some faint gold on the flanks that favour the sun. Today, apparently, is the day the enemy has chosen for its final assault, its harvest of the last pits from the last hold-outs against extermination. At the moment, anyway, the stand of apricot trees is absolutely over-run with squirrels of every colour, shape, size, and disposition, all in a frolic and frenzy: black ones, brown ones, red ones, baby ones, hugely pregnant ones, mangy ones, greedy and comically obese ones, squabbling and gambolling and fussing over the last of the fruit, or searching desperately for apricot pits among the spoilage that litters the ground. You'd think winter was about to fall like a sledgehammer. And it might as well do that, as far as His Lordship is concerned. I am sincerely concerned once more about the old boy's heart, as he is manifestly beyond apoplectic. Something inarticulate, inchoate, escapes his lips. "Good God," he next says, as if he really is about the give up the ghost. Then the poor old sod weeps. I mean he really weeps, not quite silently, occasionally giving voice to his ecstatic pain with an incoherent "*Ahhhffff!*," rather like a large dog with asthma. Heartbroken, myself, offering solace, I briefly rub against his arm as he props himself on the sill, and then, faithful *amicus curiae* that I am, I remember good old Lord Eldin.

If I had fingers, I would snap them. Over the shoulder of some middle-aged snollygoster some weeks ago in the Great Library, a law professor, I suppose, or maybe he was another judge writing a paper for the Tenth Annual International Congress on Environmental Law, I read of John Clerk, dates 1757 to 1832, the Scottish judge known as Lord Eldin. Apparently Lord Eldin preferred cats to human companionship, which is neither unreasonable nor uncommon in my experience. *They don't let you down.* Anyway, the old fellow was working at home one night when a cat fight broke out in his yard. He approached the window at the back of his dwelling and, in his most judicious and reasonable tone, asked the disputants kindly to put a garbage can lid on the noise immediately, if not sooner. My ancestors ignored him, of course, so he read them the *Riot Act*, "slowly and solemnly," this biographer says.* Perhaps the whole performance was for the neighbours, watching nervously from behind their twitching curtains, just as Osgoode Hall's neighbourhood was startled out of its lazy complacency some weeks previous when Justice Mariner beaned his unsuspecting law clerk with a running shoe in the front courtyard. In any event, the old story about Lord Eldin has given me an idea.

Many of you will enjoy personal experience of the way *felis sylvestris* sometimes paws at the papers or books on your desk. No doubt you have assumed that this is base instinct, nest-making,

---

*Editor's note: Amicus is referring to W. Forbes-Gray, in his *Some Old Scots Judges*, 1914.

perhaps, the call of the wild, or, worse, idle mischief or malice. Some will say, "He's only doing that to get attention." *Guilty, me Lud! I own up to it, absolutely.* Placing my forepaws on the *Martin's Annual Criminal Code* spread-eagled on His Lordship's desk at "Mischief to Property," section 430(3), I scrape, I scratch, I paw, I scrape, I rasp, I paw some more and then again and yet further until at last His Lordship spins around to take out his frustration on Yours Persistently Scholarly, but not before I have clawed our way back to section 67 in the *Code*:

> *67. A person who is (a) a justice, mayor or sheriff. . . , who receives notice that . . . twelve or more persons are unlawfully and riotously assembled together shall go to that place and, after approaching as near as safely he may do, if he is satisfied that a riot is in progress, shall command silence and thereupon make or cause to be made in a loud voice a proclamation in the following words or to the like effect:*

> *"Her Majesty the Queen charges and commands all persons being assembled immediately to disperse and peaceably to depart to their habitations or to their lawful business upon the pain of being guilty of an offence for which, upon conviction, they may be sentenced to imprisonment for life. GOD SAVE THE QUEEN."*

Yes, the section still exists, pretty much in the form it did in Lord Eldin's day. Of course, I do not let on that the section failed to produce any greater effect on Lord Eldin's cats than it would on human rioters. It turns out (the biographer says) that His

Lordship's cats did not disperse and peaceably depart to their habitations or to their lawful business — until he fired a pistol in their general direction. Personally, as a member of a species that some classify as vermin, I remain a strong proponent of gun control.

Will you believe me, however, if I add that His Lordship Justice Theodore Mariner takes the hint, removes himself back to the window with his *Criminal Code*, pushes the window open, now that the caulking is well and truly splintered away, and, like Moses on the mountain — or, more precisely, Ernie the Voice of Doom on Queen Street — shouts out the words of section 67 to the general astonishment of the passersby below, which at the moment include the Chief Justice and his luncheon companions, the Attorney General and his Deputy.

"Her Majesty the Queen charges and commands all persons being assembled immediately to disperse and peaceably to depart to their habitations or to their lawful business upon the pain of being guilty of an offence!"

I am told that such behaviour is known as a CLM — a career limiting move. Mind you, whose career has been most limited, his Lordship's or mine, is not immediately clear.

Then, adding to the carnival atmosphere, Leland Gaunt comes up the cobbled drive. Hearing his master's voice, he stops and looks up at us, putting a hand to his forehead, perhaps wondering if he should duck to avoid flying footwear or other projectiles. Then, reassured, he cups his ear and shouts back at us: "Pardon me?"

Mortimer has established for the jury that Josey Probert is a bencher and was a close friend of the deceased, Jeremiah Debeers.

"And, if you'll forgive me, Ms. Probert, not to sound indelicate, but the jury needs to know: Were you more than friends and colleagues?"

Josey Probert smiles sadly. "Do you mean were Jerry and I seeing each other, Mr. Mortimer? Dating?"

"Yes, please. Were you going out together, I guess the term would be?"

"No. I was — I am, I suppose — seeing someone else. A mutual friend of Jerry's, as it happens."

"And who would that be, Ms. Probert?"

"Dylan Faddaster. I met him through Jerry, actually. He's the legal affairs reporter at the *Daily Standard*."

"But was, is, your relationship with Mr. Faddaster public knowledge?"

"Well, Jerry knew, of course. But the other benchers were already nervous about Jerry and me being friends with Dylan. Because of his job, you know. So we — Dylan and I — decided to play it cool. It was our personal business, and we kept it that way."

"Did Katrina Slovenskaya know you were involved with Mr. Faddaster?"

"No. I think she thought I had my eye on Jerry."

"Members of the jury," Justice M'Gonnigle says as Gaunt springs to his scuffed Hush Puppies, "Ms. Probert cannot tell you what she thought was in somebody else's mind."

"Well, anyway, then, Ms. Probert," Mortimer continues, "you worked closely with Jerry, and I understand that you told the police you have some personal knowledge about the circumstances of his death."

Probert stands straight and tall in the box, tall, anyway, for her five-feet-one-inch stature. Not a hair is out of place, as the cliché goes. Indeed, she seems to have been to the hairdresser's expressly for this public occasion. Her nails are newly manicured, her face carefully if a little heavily made up against the ravages of entropy (yes, we can hear old Ernie out on the street a couple of hundred yards away: *"See, I have this day set thee over the nations and over the kingdoms, to root out, and to pull down, and to destroy, and to throw down, to build, and to plant-a!"*), and she's smartly kitted out in a beige suit trimmed with black around its exaggerated collar — a little like a fashionable Pagliacci. It turns out, in fact, that this is a bit of archetypal casting in our melodrama. "Yes, sir. I was one of the people who found his body."

Rhubarb rhubarb rhubarb. The jury and spectators bestir themselves, leaning forward in their seats. Finally, something really interesting is happening.

"But the police evidence has been that Ms. Slovenskaya found the body, along with a library user she was assisting," Mortimer prods.

"Actually, Ms. Slovenskaya and I found Jerry the night before that."

This causes a greater commotion in the room, stimulating Her Honour Justice M'Gonnigle sternly to call for quiet. When this doesn't achieve the desired effect, her clerk steps in, the two of them scowling in opposite directions across the well of the court. Court

Clerk Level ɪᴠ Conchita Presenkowski has distracted a great many jurors and witnesses in her day, and boasts her own unofficial admirers' club among the male criminal law bar. I have heard rumours that she is the top hit on the Internet website *dishycourtstaff.com*, run by a couple of articling students who clearly are insufficiently occupied by those responsible for training at their law firms. To put it bluntly, anyway, from her admirers' point of view Conchita is the perfect moggy, a delicious multicultural blend of Poland and Venezuela, multi-hemispherically hot and cold like apple pie with Häagen Dazs ice cream, slender but fully endowed in both her hemispheres; pale but freckled on her generously displayed skin; round-faced but with flawless if pallid epidermis and prominent, rubescent cheekbones that give her an aspect of something just-ripe juicy, or a femme fatale out of traditional ballad; that sweetly dangerous mien framed by honey-blonde hair, with natural, heatherish, kittenish streaks of auburn and chocolate all through it. *Glory be to God for dappled things.* And she's more than a bit of a dominatrix, besides. "Quiet!" Conchita shouts, and it is like the thwack of a horsewhip. Her wish is everyone's command.

With the room restored to its accustomed hush, Gaunt remains poker-faced, and poor homely Katrina Slovenskaya stares at her hands, making herself look as guilty as Lady MacBeth, and more alone in the prisoner's dock than ever. *Double, double, toil and trouble. Fire burn, and cauldron bubble.*

"Please elaborate on that for the jury," Mortimer continues, placid, but raising his eyebrows at the jurors as though he's about to show them an especially clever card trick. "About finding the body."

"Well, Jerry and I had discovered that bottles were going missing from the Law Society's wine cellar. Or rather, that there were various unexplained losses from inventory, and some suspicious food expenditures, too, for the kitchen and what-not, various items that were not fully accounted for. So we were doing a little undercover investigation. Jerry chaired the Hospitality Committee, you see, and I'm co-chair with Treasurer Fitz-Niblick of the Finance Committee."

"Yes. Go on, please."

"Well, you're not supposed to remove the log from the wine cellar, the Treasurer is very strict about that, and he's a big wine enthusiast, so he sniffs around down there himself quite a lot."

"By log, you mean the inventory record for the wine cellar?"

"Yes, what liquor comes in and what goes out. The record. So anyway, we — Jerry and I — we didn't want anyone to know we were snooping around. We didn't want to put any culprits on their guard, if you see what I mean, because we hoped to catch them at it red-handed. But we wanted to preserve the evidence, so we decided to photocopy the log."

"To track what was coming in and going out?"

"Exactly. So, while Jerry chaired the meeting of the Hospitality Committee and kept everyone busy — typically the kitchen management came to the meetings, see — so while they were in the meeting, I was supposed to do the photocopying. Jerry had the key to the cellar, and he was supposed to leave the log in the Journals Room at the library, where I was going to photocopy it."

"When were you going to do that?"

"Well, as I say, while the Hospitality Committee was meeting. After the library was officially closed. Katrina was supposed to let me in."

"But this was on a Sunday?"

"Yes. The Hospitality Committee often met on Sundays so that the members didn't have to take out time from their regular workdays. Jerry usually didn't come for the Sunday meetings, but he made an exception this time, so we could do the photocopying. That's how he planned it, anyway. He said there would be fewer people in the building while I used the machine. The plan was, Katrina was meeting Jerry for dinner, I guess, after his meeting. And she was waiting for him in the library, and so she was going to let me in. She has her own keys, of course."

"I see."

"But it turned out I was early. I mean, I was already in the library. I got there before the weekend staff locked up for the day, and I was doing some of my work, from my law practice, in the reading room, on the main floor — the second floor."

"You were already in the library, but you hadn't seen Ms. Slovenskaya at that point?"

"Correct. And I was just doing some of my own work at that time because, for one thing, I didn't think Jerry would have been in with the log yet. And I had to, you know, top up the credit on my photocopy card and all that. I needed like thirty dollars worth or more, because there was a lot to copy."

"From the log."

"Yes, from the log."

"So then what happened?"

"Well, the library staff locked up and I decided to go downstairs, where they wouldn't see me and get suspicious. Also, Jerry had told me there was something wrong with the outlet for the photocopier down there. The plug was always coming out, he said, so you had to jiggle it, or push it in before you started copying.

Otherwise, everything might short out on you, and your copies would get stuck in the machine. And then we'd get found out. But it was still the best machine to use, he said, because it was secluded down there."

"On the first floor, below the main entrance and the reading room?"

"Right. So I thought I'd better get going and check all that, the plug and everything. I was nervous about getting all the copying done without anyone finding out. The records are confidential, as I say, and the log's not supposed to leave the cellar. And then I met Katrina in the corridor, just outside the fire door."

"Which corridor do you mean?"

"The one on the first floor there. One floor down. Just outside the Journals Room."

"And did you say anything to Katrina?"

"Well, she was surprised that I was already there, of course. We got to chatting. She seemed a bit distracted, though. Sort of in a hurry to get away or something."

Gaunt slowly rises. "Your Honour, that's conclusory, or at best speculative."

"Members of the jury," Justice M'Gonnigle says. "Again, the witness cannot tell you how Ms. Slovenskaya felt or what she thought."

"But she can say how she looked, Your Honour," Mortimer replies.

The judge arches her eyebrows, nods, and says, "Fair enough, Mr. Mortimer."

"She looked distracted," Probert says, glancing grimly at the accused, "and sort of red-faced."

"And then what?" Mortimer asks.

"Well, we heard this loud popping, or a bang, I guess. And it sounded like it came from somewhere just inside the door. Katrina said it was probably nothing. An old building is like an old man, she said. It makes rude noises in the night."

Another stern look from Conchita squelches the scattered amusement. Two men on the jury — one a middle-aged, paunchy sort, the other, a young buck with greasy, black hair — actually blush and squirm, the smiles not quite leaving their faces.

"So what did you do then?"

"Well, I went through the fire door and looked anyway, and Katrina was trailing along after me like a nervous hen, and we heard another bang. A really loud one, this time. Definitive. And it was obvious that it came from the Journals Room. And then, well, then we found poor Jerry." The witness shrugs, the blood drains from her face and her eyes go vacant as she follows her mind back in time to the Journals Room that fateful evening.

"And did you call for help?"

The witness Probert returns to the present and the land of the living. "Well, we thought about it, of course. But we could tell he was already gone. We didn't see any wounds or anything, so I checked his breathing, and there was nothing. We assumed he'd had a heart attack. I mean, we didn't touch him or anything. I had my mirror, my compact mirror. And I held it near his mouth, you know, the way they do in the movies."

"And third-rate detective novels," the judge says, smiling at the jury.

"Well, we weren't sure what else to do, in the situation. It was plastic, see, so it was safe. I mean, with the electricity and all that.

And then we started talking about it, Katrina and I, and the more we talked, the more panicky we got, I guess. I mean, it all looked so sneaky and suspicious. Worse than it really was. We realized that Katrina would get into trouble for letting us in there, and also we'd have to explain what we were doing there and it would compromise everything that Jerry and I had been trying to do. Our little undercover investigation, I mean. It would completely blow our cover and all that. Katrina and I would have been in a bit of a mess. So we decided to just leave it until the next day, to avoid further harm. I mean, in retrospect, it was incredibly stupid."

"Yes," Mortimer agrees.

"But poor Jerry was gone." The witness shakes and bows her head. "And we left in the heat of it all. And once we were out of there, well, it seemed like there was no going back. We were stuck with our stupid choice. Because whatever we did, we'd just make it even worse. It was like what they say about quicksand, you know? The more you struggle, the deeper you sink. I mean, it's not exactly great for a bencher to be charged with obstructing justice, is it?" Josey Probert sighs and shakes her head.

"So what did you do after you left the Journals Room?"

"Well. It sounds really cold and awful. But as I say, we were rattled and scared, and we thought it would look best, in case anybody saw us, for us to go have some tea or something. So, you know, it would look like Katrina was just meeting me at the library for that reason, and nothing was wrong. And, anyway, we needed to talk, calm each other down and think things through."

"Get your stories straight."

The witness grimaces and considers Mortimer's remark, then admits, "Well, yes. I wouldn't like to put it that way, but that's what it comes down to. Figure out what to do, what to say, and all that. We were terribly upset, of course, and we didn't want to be alone. We needed the mutual support, if nothing else."

"So did you leave the library?"

"Well, not right away. Because there was this Tupperware box on the floor, like for keeping your leftovers or lunch in or something. It was near Jerry's legs — his knee. I didn't see it very well, though. Katrina scooped it up before I could take it all in and, again, my mind was all over the place. But it seemed to have some wires in it, I thought. The Tupperware. Electrical wiring or something, and some tools. And we went back upstairs with that, and Katrina put it in her desk. But only after we were across the street at the hotel, having tea and trying to calm each other down, well, it wasn't until then that we remembered the log. And we were too scared to go back for it. It was too late."

"And did you ever tell the police about any of this?"

"Well, yes. After they charged Katrina, she told them we were together that evening. I mean, it came out, and the police charged me with obstructing justice and mischief." For the first time, Probert's composure genuinely breaks, and she looks at the floor, biting her lip. Recovering herself, she smiles sadly and says, "So I was in trouble anyway. It was all for nothing, and we did just make it worse after all. But then you offered to withdraw the charges, Mr. Mortimer, if I agreed to give evidence here today, and to resign as bencher."

A tear runs down her cheek, but Josey keeps her gaze evenly on Crown counsel, eyes wide, shoulders straight, a good soldier.

"Yes, I think the jury should hear that from us, thank you, Ms. Probert."

"Your Honour." Gaunt thrusts himself up on his hockey-stick hind legs. "The jury may rest assured that they were going to hear it in any event. We certainly were not going to let that escape their attention. Not for love, as Mr. Mortimer has put it, money — or plea bargains."

"Yes, yes, Mr. Gaunt," Justice M'Gonnigle says as Mortimer opens his maw to its full extent, preparing to howl at the midday sun. "And I imagine that you might be bringing it to their attention again before we're finished here."

Before Gaunt can respond, Mortimer begins, "We are indeed seeking to withdraw those charges against Ms. Probert, Your Honour," when his witness breaks in.

"Well, it's all been very painful for me, Your Honour, even so." Josey Probert puts her hand to her mouth and is briefly mute, then haltingly adds, with another teary smile, "I'd like to say that publicly, before the court and the jury." She bows her head a little and flutters her eyelids at the twelve citizens good and true in the box to her right. "I very much regret my mistakes. They were not meant to cause harm. I only meant to do the right thing. I've lost everything, you know." She sniffles and pauses again. "Even though I'm not charged now. It's very trying. Sad and trying." Probert smiles bravely up at the Court. "I mean, I could even be disbarred from the practice of law. It's very trying."

Only figuratively for you, my dear, I mutter, *compared to poor old Katrina Daniella Slovenskaya.*

"But here I am," says former bencher Probert. "I've come forward, to try to make things right. Here I am, Your Honour."

And there you go.

"Order to go," Her Honour nods at the witness and then at the redoubtable Conchita Presenkowski, who glances obediently up at the bench, "dismissing the charges against Ms. Probert."

"Thank you kindly, Your Honour," Mortimer says.

CHAPTER 4

Old Boys, New Girls

They say that 175 years ago it was the repository of one of the most pre-eminent backsides in Canada. For most of the 33 years that he was chief justice, it provided institutional support to the very white, Anglo-Saxon *gluteus maximus* of Sir John Beverley Robinson, former attorney-general and president of the executive council of Upper Canada. In a long silk robe trimmed with ermine, pale-faced, thin, a little dyspeptic, and not obviously grateful for life's bounty as a big fish in nineteenth-century British North America (as he liked to call it) — looking, in other words, like Whistler's Grumpy Mother — the Anglican paternalist is portrayed in sombre oils as he sits larger than life in the *fauteuil* in question, portentously gilt-framed above the massive fireplace in the main reading room of the Hall's Great Library. It is truly pride of place: His Lordship surveys one of the most awe-inspiring rooms in the country.

On a brass plaque set in a pedestal below the portrait, the Historic Sites and Monuments Board of Canada provides Sir John's résumé:

Sir John Beverley Robinson, Baronet, 1791–1863

The son of Loyalists, . . . John Beverley Robinson was the embodiment of the values of the early Upper Canadian Tories known as the Family Compact. . . . A defender of British institutions, of the rights of rank and property and of an established church, he was also an early proponent of British North America union.

What the plaque doesn't say is that the term "Family Compact" is derisory. It is meant to signal that Robinson and his Establishment cronies ran the province like their private old boys' club. In fact, in what some might view today as a classic conflict of interest, as attorney-general and former Law Society treasurer he sold the society the land on which its Osgoode Hall headquarters currently stands.

By 1837 the more democratically minded got fed up at all the *noblesse oblige* and staged a darkly comical rebellion. As evening fell one day in early December, they marched down Yonge Street, brandishing guns, sticks, and pitchforks to confront the loyalist Compact forces. The loyalists fired a volley at the rebels, then skittered off. The rebels in the front line returned fire, then dropped to the ground to allow their fellows to fire the next round over them. But thinking their leaders had been decimated, the rebels fled back north. Sir John had two of them executed, and Osgoode Hall became the loyalists' garrison.

History, it seems, repeats itself. The current chair-owner, anyway, now towers over said antiquity at his full WASPish height, or above it, lifted onto his toes by rage and other unhealthy emotions, dangerously red-faced with all that blood flooding into his

face and throbbing veins as he wails, "Why?" Job, he seems, rein-
carnate at Osgoode Hall. His wife and daughters (the oboist and
the Bay Street corporate lawyer) bought the historic chair at auction on the occasion of his appointment to the Court of Appeal,
for installation in his new chambers at Osgoode Hall. And His
Lordship Justice Mariner had it reupholstered "on authentic his-
torical principles" at considerable added expense

"Why?" Life's eternal question is repeated yet more despair-
ingly, and there follow many threats and imprecations, only some
of which I take in, try as I might to deafen myself to them all as I
skitter out of chambers and down the corridor. There, I pass an
equally skittish Leland Gaunt coming the other way, or rather,
standing stock-still, flattened against the wall like a cat burglar, listening wide-eyed to the ruckus, his mouth slightly ajar, nervous of
his personal safety in the circumstances. *Yes, it's probably best not
to disturb His Lordship just now,* I advise as I streak by. And just
before I turn the corner for the stairway we both hear from judge's
chambers yet another, yet more plaintive, "Why?"

So melancholy is the query, so beggarly the question, that it
stops me in my tracks. *Why not?* I turn and reply. It is the only reasonable answer. Stretched stiff on its filigreed hem and anchored
into the hardwood with some 176 brass rivets (I know, I've counted
and recounted as I lay there many times in my contemplative bore-
dom and somnolence), the chair's red leather seat was hard,
inflexible and downright frigid on the haunches and belly. No wonder our Sir John was such a miserable old Tory! Surely Leland Gaunt
has thought that, too, perched there anxiously during his many
painful meetings with his judicial master. And there was all that soft
batting so easily accessible just a quarter of an inch beneath, the

plush cotton stuffing so much better suited to mammalian repose, no matter your particular species or the configuration of your personal haunch. I mean, I thought long and hard before shredding that leather seat, didn't I? And I don't see how you can be convicted of violating your probation if you're acting in the community's best interests. It seemed like a good idea at the time, anyway.

Mortimer coughs loudly, waking me from where I doze at the feet of the nubile yet redoubtable Conchita Presenkowski, having once more escaped judgment myself before Theodore Elisha Mariner, Justice of Appeal. I figure His Lordship can't exactly charge me with evading lawful custody if I'm sitting just up the street in the Superior Court, exercising my public right to open justice while keeping a gimlet eye on his mousy law clerk. "Ms. Probert," Mortimer is droning on, "I'd like to take you now to the corporation."

Oh good, a field trip, far away from judicial wrath.

"Other witnesses have told the jury that Mr. Debeers incorporated a company with his mother as a director. Do you know anything about that?"

"Well, Jerry and I often used the same paralegal clerk." The hard part done, the witness is almost perky. "Satish Sengupta. I ran into Satish one day, in the lobby outside the commercial list courts. And he mentioned to me that he'd just done the incorporation for that particular business. It was just by way of making conversation. Public record stuff. He didn't violate any confidences."

"And did you discuss that with Mr. Debeers?"

"Well, I mentioned it to him. I said I'd seen Satish and that he'd told me that was why he was in the building. Doing an incorporation for Jerry. But Jerry wasn't very chatty about it, either. He shrugged it off. Apparently it was just some sort of investment vehicle for his mother's retirement funds."

"That's what you understood it to be, an investment vehicle for her retirement funds?

"Yes. That's all I know about it."

Mortimer's fanny has not hit his chair before Leland Gaunt is on his feet and immediately on the attack. "Mr. Debeers wasn't very popular with the other benchers, was he, Ms. Probert?"

"Well, he was a bit of a gadfly. As I've described, he was fighting for the little guy. And gal, of course."

"I suppose we'll see about that. He had a nickname among the benchers, didn't he?"

"Yes. They called him the Splinter."

"Because he was a bit of a pain in the behind, isn't that right?"

The jury laughs, glancing nervously at Conchita, who this time lets it pass. It is all part of her clerkly, sex-kitten, dominatrix contradictions, the locus of her power: keep them guessing.

"I don't know. Something like that, I suppose."

"And they even joked about various ways of doing him in, didn't they? Various ways of eliminating him, or dare I say killing him?"

"Really, Mr. Gaunt. That was just fooling around."

"Really, Ms. Probert. Except now that he's been fried to death, it isn't such a cute little game, is it?"

"I think that's a very crude way of putting it, Mr. Gaunt."

"Cruder than sticking poisoned umbrellas in his fanny? Cruder than sticking an icicle into his brain? Weren't those some of the so-called jokes?"

"I don't know. They didn't make them in front of me."

"But he knew about this so-called fooling around, didn't he?"

"Well, yes." The witness permits herself to titter. "The ring-leader, Dylan Faddaster, his friend, our friend, from the *Standard*, he'd report it all to Jerry, quite merrily. Play by play, as Jerry put it. Jerry liked the attention, because he thought it meant he was making some headway." Josey Probert shrugs and purses her lips at Leland Gaunt. "Getting noticed. He thought it was amusing, actually. We all laughed about it."

"Amusing. Would you call it that? Amusing?"

"I was his friend, Mr. Gaunt. You seem to be forgetting that."

"Yes, so you say, Ms. Probert. I'd like to look at that a little, actually, if you don't mind. You're telling this court that you thought Jerry Debeers had a heart attack in the library?"

"Yes. We couldn't see what else it might be. There was nothing else obvious. He just lay there."

"Yet you also just told us that you felt safe holding your compact, the mirror, up to your friend's face because it was plastic and it wouldn't conduct electricity."

"Well, I was speaking in hindsight. Now that everyone knows about the electrocution, I mean."

"Hindsight," Gaunt says. "Just like how, in hindsight, you've changed your story and worked out a deal with Mr. Mortimer? Getting yourself off the hook?"

Josey Probert chuffs and looks disgusted.

"As I understand it, you and Mr. Debeers had worked together for years as a sort of rebel rump at the Law Society. The anti-elitist fringe, or some such."

"Well, yes, something like that. We both have small practices, or had, I guess, and the Law Society's sort of a relic of the age of paternalism. The old male-dominated hierarchies. White male, I should say."

"Chauvinistic."

"Phallocratic, I think, would be more precise. It's changing a little, but really only because there's the irresistible force of multiculturalism in the whole world now. The Law Society still lags quite a bit, and we'd been trying to make it a little less of an old boys' network."

"How do you mean that?"

"Well, the Law Society's not just for Bay Street lawyers, after all. It's for all of us, and for the public, too. That's its mandate, to regulate the profession for the general public. It's not supposed to be a private club. We were trying to make it less so."

"That sounds very noble of you, Ms. Probert. Or could it also be bitter?"

"I don't think that's helpful, Mr. Gaunt," the judge says, leaning her chin wearily on a hand.

"And you say that as part of this great crusade of yours, Ms. Probert, you and Mr. Debeers were looking into the contracts for the food and beverage services at Osgoode Hall?"

"Well, I wouldn't call it a crusade, exactly. Jerry could get a little melodramatic and evangelistic about it. That was just his way of attracting attention to what he believed in. He managed to bring things to light, where they might otherwise stay in the shadows this big old place throws on them. That's what I mean by the old boys' network. It's entrenched. That's just a fact, Mr. Gaunt, whether I'm embittered or not."

"All right, then. So what were you managing to bring to light?"

"Well, for example, as I was saying earlier, there was some use, exploitation, I guess, of the inventory, the dining hall's food and wine, for private purposes. You know, people taking something here and there, or we thought occasionally catering their private little networking things out of the society's larder."

"Your Honour." Mortimer rises only so far as a crouch. "I think we literally are into the price of beans, here, and I fail to see what they have to do with this first-degree murder prosecution. I don't see the relevance."

Gaunt does not trouble himself to sit while Mortimer objects. Instead, he rolls his eyes at the ceiling and answers, "I would think it's obvious, Your Honour, that it's very much relevant to the question of who might have been annoyed with Mr. Debeers. Who wanted to keep him quiet, perhaps."

"Yes, Mr. Gaunt," the judge rules. "Go on."

"So you were saying, Ms. Probert, that there was theft from the hospitality inventory?"

"Well, we hadn't found anything terribly damning. Just the fact that people were occasionally raiding the wine cellar and the pantry, you know, the cookie jar, for their own use. But some fairly expensive wines had gone missing. We weren't all that worried about the chips and biscuits. It was the wine, the smoked salmon, the pâtés, that sort of thing."

"And who was doing this? Did you know?"

"Well, it seemed to be pretty widespread, but we weren't sure. In a few cases we knew names. We knew some of the dining staff was doing it on a minor scale. And it appeared that sometimes a bencher would even sign for something and take it on the pretext that he or she was using it on Law Society business. But it seemed to be private, in fact, in some cases, and the hospitality fund was not reimbursed."

"And who in particular might have been doing that?"

"As I say, it was pretty widespread. Mostly petty pilfering. I know Mr. Nobb did it a couple of times, for example. Roman Nobb."

"Anyone else?"

"Several other benchers, now and again."

"The treasurer?"

"Possibly, but I couldn't say for sure. He's quite the oenophile, as I mentioned to Mr. Mortimer."

"Quite the what?"

"Wine lover. He's very big on wines. Has his own cellar. He and Mr. Nobb are on the wine committee, as well. They choose the liquor for the cellar, along with an outside consultant. And the treasurer was a member of the Society's wine-tasting club, before we put the kibosh on that particular little perk." Probert bobbed her head with a look satisfaction, as though she were checking off a job on her to-do list.

"So you abolished the wine-tasting club?"

"Well, even its little circle of members had to admit it didn't look very good publicly, or to the rest of the legal profession, who paid for the wine. I mean, talk about an old boys' club . . ."

"And you were also looking into the food supply deals, you say? Regarding suppliers and how they were dealt with?"

"Yes, that was one of the things we were doing. We were looking into the whole hospitality mandate. The dining room and catering had been operating at a loss for years, and now we were getting even deeper into cost over-runs, with expensive public relations and supplier contracts, a five-star chef and all that."

"Whom Mr. Fitz-Niblick had brought in."

"Yes, that all came in under his mandate. And it was beginning to look more and more like a bottomless money pit."

"And so what were you proposing to do about that?"

"Some of the benchers were in favour of privatizing the whole enterprise, you know, just contracting it right out holus-bolus, putting the management of the thing in private hands and even letting the contractors or new owners rent out Convocation Hall — the dining room — for private functions. Also, just to keep the books straight, the idea was to charge the benchers for their use of the dining services — you know, they were already using it, so why not make it pay? But we were against all that, Jerry and I, because, again, it would have worked to the profit of a few without real input from the profession."

"You and Jerry opposed privatization?"

"We were resisting the privatization, at least until we had a clearer picture of what was going on. We were trying to show that we could regulate things ourselves. The benchers, I mean."

"Correct me if I'm wrong, Ms. Probert, but if you discovered that benchers and staff were misconducting themselves with the supplies — taking things without paying for them and what have you — and if you suspected that the staff and benchers were making bad deals with suppliers and generally not managing the thing properly, well, wouldn't those be arguments *for* privatization, not against it? Wouldn't that suggest that the benchers could *not* be trusted to regulate themselves?"

"Well, not necessarily. I mean, it would be an argument for better oversight. Better controls by us as benchers."

"But also possibly for privatization?"

"Well, I guess you could use it that way."

"And Dylan Faddaster, the legal affairs reporter at the *Standard*, he was helping you do this looking into things, as you put it?"

"Well, as someone close to us, he was using the paper's resources, you know, and their contacts, to do a little digging, yes. Into the various suppliers. Their corporate records and all that."

"Someone close to you. In fact, you had introduced him to the paralegal clerk you use, Mr. Sengupta, isn't that correct? And Mr. Sengupta was helping Mr. Faddaster with the corporate searches of the suppliers of the food and drink and other services?"

"Well, yes."

"But Jerry didn't want anyone else involved like that, did he? Not even Mr. Sengupta?"

"No. He thought the fewer people involved the better. He wanted it hush-hush, so that we could do it all undercover, without the secret slipping out — you know, without blowing our cover. He didn't really trust Dylan, but I did, of course, and I trusted Satish, as well. We've worked with him for years, in many solicitor-client situations. Confidential, I mean. And we needed the help."

"And was Satish against privatizing the hospitality services at Osgoode Hall, just like you and Jerry?"

"Well, I don't know if he had an opinion on it. He's not actually a lawyer, of course. He was just assisting."

"What if I were to tell you that Jerry Debeers was actually in favour of privatization?"

"I'd say you were wrong."

"Dead wrong?"

"Please, Mr. Gaunt," Justice M'Gonnigle scowls at Gaunt as though he is a naughty schoolboy, and shakes her head in mock disgust. "Let's just stick to the facts."

"Absolutely, Your Honour. Perfect, in fact. Ms. Probert, what if I were to tell you not only that Jerry Debeers was in favour of privatizing the hospitality mandate, as you call it, but that he wanted a piece of the action, himself?"

"I'd say you were dragging the name of a decent man through the mud, Mr. Gaunt."

"I hope my friend has some evidence to back up his mud-slinging," Mortimer throws in, deliberately breaking the tension. Or adding to it, depending on your point of view.

"Sit down, please, Mr. Mortimer," Her Honour replies, throwing her pen on her notepad.

"I certainly hope that I am not dragging the name of a good man through the mud, Ms. Probert." Gaunt leans forward, pausing to gaze around the room in a fashion he no doubt imagines to be a sort of pregnant flourish. "But just assume for the moment that I'm right. It would have made you very angry, wouldn't it, for Jerry Debeers to be publicly stating he was against privatization, and then going behind your back to get his finger into that particular pie, as it were — using all the inside information you were helping him collect to privatize the thing for himself?"

"Well, I'd be very disappointed."

"Disappointed? You'd be enraged, in fact, wouldn't you?"

"Well, I don't know about that."

"After you've worked years with Jerry Debeers to make the Law Society less of an old boys' network, I think you said, less elitist, and he exploits just that sort of insider relationship for his own profit? Stabs you in the back with the same knife he's using on that big fat piece of old boys' pie? Uses you to set it all up. And you wouldn't be enraged?"

"I'd certainly feel quite shocked and annoyed."

"Quite? And quite embittered? Betrayed?"

"And betrayed."

"Yes, of course you would. I bet you would."

CHAPTER 5

Conflict of Interest

Of course, the essence of privatization is often that it is garishly public: like the streetwalker in hot pants, the success of an enterprise generally depends on how popular it becomes. Consider what became of Levy's Deli.

It was after old man Levy died that I fell in with the populist hip-grunge-fringe scene as exemplified by Murray "Moishe" Feldman and Mark Fukuhama, dropouts from the biochemistry and philosophy programs, respectively, at the University of Toronto. They bought the deli from Mrs. Levy and "funked it up" or, as they eventually described it, "grunged it down," by inviting friends and passersby in for a party and letting them paint whatever they liked on the walls. The PR value of this anarchic approach to commerce proved enormous, and Tokyo Moishe's Kosher-Oriental Deli was off to a running start. Like Ben and Jerry of caring-capitalist ice cream fame, Feldman and Fukuhama projected classic movies on the back wall in the alley behind the store, sponsored open-stage nights for amateur musicians, and donated their daily leftovers to orphanages and other shelters for the needy. Within a few years, Tokyo Moishe's was a North

American chain, with feelers in Europe and Asia. "We were the original fusion cuisine," Feldman once told a business magazine writer. "Barely controlled fusion. Truly nuclear. Chaos theory in action."

The partners became press darlings for using their supposed counterculture roots (pure fantasy, I can now disclose, given that both lived comfortably with their parents during school and for the first year or so of business) to "grunge down" business administration into a form of market-driven tumult. Image, or the mocking of it — the slapdash decor, the ever-evolving hand-scrawled menus, the indifferent waitresses in torn hip-huggers and dirty, indifferently buttoned blousons, the "world music" concerts every Sunday brunch — was everything. Tokyo Moishe's signs, spouting pretentious puns as relics of the partners' brush with academe, became especially notorious. Although I don't recall eels ever featuring on the menu, they had hung a big sign over the front door reading, in Hebrew-style typography: "O tempura! O morays! It's time for Japanese!" And apparently it was, with a little chicken soup and eggroll to start. Another placard, over the fridge where they kept the sushi and smoked salmon, announced, "Cheapest fish plates in town! After all, we don't even bother to cook it!" The Levys would have *plotzed*.

Eventually it all became too much like work. Mark Fukuhama sold out to Moishe Feldman and went off to study mystical Judaism in California. Moishe Feldman, looking prosperous from his years of sampling the inventory, became even richer by expanding into real estate development — condominiums and lofts, especially. But that, as they say, is another kettle of fishiness.

∽◌◌◌∼

"Mr. Fitz-Niblick," Gaunt asks his first witness for the defence, "as treasurer of the Law Society, what can you tell us about this move to privatize the dining hall, the catering, and such?"

"Well, I'm in favour of it. Very vocally, in fact." The witness smiles at the jury, his spectacles flashing, daring them to object. "It's been a sort of pet project of mine. I've promoted it, you see, because routinely we've been in the red in that area, and we've felt sure that it is a part of our operations which would perform better if it were run by people with the relevant expertise."

"How have you proposed that the privatizing will work?"

"Well, without wishing to be rude, Mr. Gaunt, I have to say I'm afraid that's confidential information. Also, you'll excuse me for saying I just don't think it has anything to do with this proceeding, with respect."

"And with respect, I think that's for Her Honour to decide, Mr. Fitz-Niblick."

"Your Honour," Mortimer says. "It's his witness, and he knows he's not supposed to treat him like that."

"Hang on," Justice M'Gonnigle says. "First of all, Mr. Fitz-Niblick, Mr. Gaunt is right. I'll rule on what evidence gets in and what evidence does not get in. Second, Mr. Gaunt, Mr. Fitz-Niblick is your witness. Last I heard, we don't go at our own witnesses with hammer and tongs."

"Certainly not, Your Honour, and I apologize to the witness for my tone, if it was unintentionally offensive. I was just pointing out the procedure, just as Your Honour stated it."

"Toadying, sonny boy," Mortimer grumbles over the hand propping up his chin.

"The treasurer well knows the procedure, Mr. Gaunt," the judge replies, nodding and smiling at the elegant little man in the box, then glaring at Justice Mariner's scrawny and unkempt clerk. "Particularly now that he has been reminded by the both of us."

Reddening, and no more steady on his feet than usual, Gaunt tries again. "To understand the context of Mr. Debeers' unfortunate end, Mr. Fitz-Niblick, I think the jury needs to know some context about his role on the hospitality committee."

"Now he's making speeches," Mortimer objects.

"He's asking a question, Mr. Mortimer. I don't see the harm. Stop sniping, please. We all see where he's going."

"I see where he's going, Your Honour," the witness says, "and I can only say that we were intending to contract out the hospitality services. Assuming that we could win the vote on our privatization scheme. Among the benchers, I mean. And that's it. I was for it. Jerry Debeers was ag'in it. End of story."

"But isn't it really just the beginning, Mr. Fitz-Niblick?" Gaunt presses on. "What I'm asking you, sir, is how you intended to do all that in light of the opposition, such as Jerry Debeers'."

The treasurer shrugs and burbles, grinning helplessly at the jury. "By the usual procedures you normally use in business, Mr. Gaunt. Lobbying to get the other benchers to agree to it. Then taking tenders, offers, for the contract, sir, which the benchers would all review."

"Offers from whom?"

"As I've told you, Mr. Gaunt, that's confidential. It's just garden-variety business. Private Law Society business. It would compromise everything to make it public. And anyway, you needn't worry yourself about it. It has nothing to do with who killed poor Jerry Debeers, I assure you."

"Ah, but that's just it, Mr. Fitz-Niblick. How do you know that? How do you know that it has nothing to do with who killed Jerry Debeers?"

"Well, if I told you that, it wouldn't be confidential any more, would it?"

Gaunt asks the judge to remove the jury and Fitz-Niblick. When they have filed out, he applies to treat the treasurer as a hostile witness.

"Can we really say he's hostile, Mr. Gaunt, after two or three questions not quite on topic?" Justice M'Gonnigle rests her cheek in her hand, peering again over the top of her glasses at defence counsel.

"Well, at least adverse, entitling me to cross-examine him, Your Honour." Gaunt's tone becomes plaintive. "And entitling me to raise a reasonable doubt as to the guilt of Ms. Slovenskaya. I mean, Mr. Debeers was a man of quite some controversy, after all. The questions are more on topic than they might seem. And he's stonewalling."

"Mr. Gaunt." The court sits up straight and purses her lips, annoyed like a mother with her whining child. "This is not a melodrama, and the gentleman in question is the treasurer of our law society. And the treasurer is not on trial here for his business dealings."

"Or anything else, come to that," Mortimer adds.

"Or anything else." The judge nods. "I mean, we seem to be getting into the price of beans, again, or at least the fact that these questions have nothing to do with that price."

"Well, Your Honour, in my respectful submission, they do. That's what I'm trying to convey here." Gaunt shifts his weight and cocks his jaw in that discomfiting, double-jointed way of his. "In my submission, we have questionable activity here, questionable secret business dealings, and I'd submit that you don't know where such things can lead. I would venture to say that they might even lead to violence among the partners. I mean, who knows? Or at least there certainly must have been bad feelings in the air at some of the meetings. Heated meetings on the issue, as we've all read, among people who didn't get along all that well in the first place. So who knows where it might all have led?"

"And pigs might fly, Mr. Gaunt," the judge remarks, then throws up her hands and shrugs, her slender arms barely visible in the archangel wings of her black robe. "But then again, who am I to say? One sees everything from the bench, much of it incredible, much of it regrettable, particularly as it concerns man's inhumanity to man. I'm going to grant the application. But I'm going to watch your winged pig like a hungry hawk."

"He'd better be doing more than hamming it up, Your Honour," Mortimer adds with a simpering bow, thrilled to little mint balls with his joke. "Inflaming the jury's appetite to lay blame where it doesn't belong. Accusing Mr. Fitz-Niblick of pork-barrelling, no doubt."

"You think that's a joke, Mr. Mortimer?" Gaunt asks, fronting his opponent with a look of honest curiosity, and then turning to the judge with a genuinely amusing attempt to look flabbergasted.

Once the jury is re-empanelled, Gaunt begins a cross-examination of his own witness, Treasurer Samuel Fitz-Niblick. "Now

Mr. Fitz-Niblick, as treasurer or head of the Law Society you're an important player in a colourful and celebrated history, aren't you?"

"I like to think so, Mr. Gaunt," the witness agrees, smiling and nodding at the jury. "It's an honour of historic lineage, and I do my best to merit it."

"For instance, Sir John Beverley Robinson was treasurer, wasn't he? One of the principals in the Family Compact?"

"Back in the earliest days, yes, the 1830s I think it was. And he went on to be chief justice for many years, and he was very prominent in Canadian politics."

Mortimer turns his big, goateed head to the jury, plunks it in his right hand, snorts, and extravagantly rolls his eyes before closing them on Gaunt's history lesson. Justice M'Gonnigle permitting, it appears that he would snore, as well.

"Indeed he did," Gaunt says. "He was very much an Establishment man, wasn't he? Landed gentry, really."

"Indeed, sir, he was. What the British call a toff."

"Yes, he was rather British at the time, wasn't he? A loyalist."

"A loyalist, yes."

"Antirevolutionary, anti-American. And not all that democratic."

"Well, there were those who said so. I mean, yes, he was part of what amounted to the colonial aristocracy, loyal to the British motherland, and some people resented that. But these were the early days of our society, and, unlike the United States, we had thrown our lot in with the Brits. Besides, you always have your grumble-guts, don't you, in any society? There was the 1837 rebellion, of course, a sort of limited people's revolution against him and the powers that were."

"And he had two of the rebels executed, didn't he?"

"Your Honour," Mortimer finally moans into his hand, without opening his eyes or bothering to stand. "Some of us have already done history at school, and Mr. Gaunt is again forgetting the price of beans. Very stale ones, at this point."

"Just where are you heading here, Mr. Gaunt," the judge asks, "if anywhere in the last two centuries?"

"Well, Your Honour, I just want to ask the treasurer if, on top of all that sort of let-them-eat-cake business, isn't it true, Treasurer, that your forebear Sir John sold the Law Society the land it occupies today — what we now call Osgoode Hall, just down the street?"

"The land, I believe he did, yes. For one thousand pounds, I've read."

"But he was attorney general at the time, wasn't he? And, as we've agreed, a former treasurer of the Law Society?"

"I'd have to check my history book on that, Mr. Gaunt. I'll take your word for it."

"Well, even if he wasn't attorney general, if he was a former treasurer and went on to be chief justice for thirty-three years and at the same time he sells land to his own professional body, wouldn't you call that a conflict of interest? Selling something to his own law society for personal gain?"

Mortimer's eyes fly open. "Your Honour," he bellows, manfully struggling to bring his nicotine-stained bulk erect, "this is all very interesting, but I believe it really is ancient, not to say musty, history and quite beside the point."

"The point I'm trying to make, Your Honour," Gaunt replies, pouting a little, "is precisely that it is not. Ancient, I mean. History. It's taking place here and now and it's right on point."

"Just get to that point, then, Mr. Gaunt," the judge rules. "Here and now. We can all watch *Canada, A People's History* on television at home."

"Okay, then, Treasurer. Isn't it true that you wanted to sell something to Osgoode Hall, just like old Sir John? Isn't it true that you set up your own corporation to run the hospitality services at Osgoode Hall?"

"Well, it wasn't just my corporation. And of course we were going to bring in experts to do the actual planning and catering. To run the services."

"And when you say 'we,' whom do you mean?"

"I mean the shareholders, Mr. Nobb and myself, as well as Mr. Debeers, his friend Mr. Feldman, and a couple of minor shareholders. There. Now you know, Mr. Gaunt. Congratulations. And now you can see that it's completely irrelevant and useless here."

"Yet when the police asked you about who the shareholders were, you said you didn't know."

"I think you'll find that I told them what I told you, Mr. Gaunt. I told them that I couldn't say. It was confidential, after all, as I keep explaining to you, so I simply told them I couldn't say."

"How very lawyerly of you, Treasurer. In other words, you left them with the impression that you didn't know."

"I'm not responsible for their impressions, Mr. Gaunt, am I?"

"Did the minor shareholders include the accused, Ms. Slovenskaya?"

"Yes, after some debate, she became the smallest shareholder, I believe. Mr. Debeers brought her in, as a trustworthy director."

"Trustworthy, you say?" Gaunt turns briefly toward the jury box. "And Mr. Debeers, was he a major shareholder or minor?"

"Sort of middling."

"Fifteen per cent to the sixty held by you and Mr. Nobb, isn't that correct?"

"Yes. I hold thirty per cent and my colleague Roman Nobb holds thirty."

"And you call fifteen versus sixty middling?"

"Well, Debeers wasn't major, and he wasn't as minor as some. And of course, his own mother held another seven per cent."

"And Ms. Slovenskaya held three?"

"I believe that's correct, yes."

"She and Mrs. Debeers were directors, but they were the smallest shareholders?"

"Yes, yes, Mr. Gaunt. Yes."

"But really they didn't direct much of anything, did they?"

"No. It's just pro forma. A common business practice. You name certain individuals, who in fact don't necessarily do much day to day."

"You use them."

"I wouldn't say that, Mr. Gaunt. They have their proper function. At annual meetings and the like. It's the conventional thing."

"Conventional. You mean the rest of the shareholders hide behind them?"

"Not exactly."

"Allow them to take the blame?"

"Only if they are in fact to blame for something."

"Really? They're not named 'pro forma,' as you put it, to serve as sacrificial lambs, to use the sort of biblical metaphor so beloved of Jerry Debeers — to use them as scapegoats, maybe, to protect the unnamed shareholders?"

"Hardly, sir. No business could run like that."

"True enough, sir. Normally a business couldn't. Unless the business depended on sacrificial lambs and scapegoats."

"Scapegoats for what, for goodness' sake?"

"I don't know, Mr. Fitz-Niblick. How about fraud? Then again, how about murder?"

After Conchita Presenkowski cracks her horsewhip, Justice M'Gonnigle warns: "Mr. Gaunt, if you want those highly prejudicial questions to stand, you'd better have a lot of evidence to show us first. To back them up. Personally, members of the jury, I think defence counsel might be going somewhat off the rails here."

"Your Honour," Mortimer adds, pro forma, it would seem, "the Crown's position will be that you will need to give the jury another warning about this, in your charge to them, after evidence closes."

"I'll withdraw the question, Your Honour," Gaunt retreats, bowing slightly. "Let me ask you instead, Treasurer: You're pretty friendly with Mr. Nobb, I take it? Roman Nobb, your fellow bencher?"

Mortimer is on his hind legs again, panting and red with the exertion. "Your Honour, I don't see what that has to do with beans, bread, or dessert, whether he's cross-examining or not."

"Your Honour," Gaunt replies, "again it has very much to do with the price of beans, not to mention wine, canapés, and bencher dinners."

"Yes, now that we understand the context, I think it might be relevant, Mr. Mortimer," Justice M'Gonnigle rules contemplatively. "Let's see where he's going."

"Yes," the treasurer agrees, "Roman Nobb and I are great friends. Anything wrong with that, as well, Mr. Gaunt? We've both been lawyers, colleagues, in this city for nearly four decades."

"But neither of you much cared for Jerry Debeers."

"Well, we didn't see him socially, if that's what you mean. One meets and works with all sorts of people in daily life. One can hold different views than they do and still work with them perfectly well. I work with you, too, for instance, don't I, Mr. Gaunt?"

"But you joked about murdering Jerry Debeers, didn't you?"

The treasurer looks deliberately amused and disgusted all at once, shaking his head, dismissing the question with a wave so that the jury gets a good look at the big diamond in the gold wedding ring on his fat little brown hand. "You said it yourself, sir. Jokes. They were jokes. How silly of you to even bring it up."

"Many a true word is spoken in jest, no, Treasurer?"

"My God, man, why on earth would I want Jerry actually dead?" The treasurer keeps smiling, but tightly, and his face has gone all mottled. "That's insane. He was my business partner, in a new undertaking. You just said so yourself."

"Quite. And speaking of that particular business arrangement — the corporation in which you and your friends were taking over the dining hall operations. Was this endorsed by the rest of the benchers? With three benchers being shareholders of the corporation, one of them publicly saying that privatization was anathema to him?"

"No. They were unaware of who the shareholders were. It was a numbered company, because we didn't want to give the impression that we were in a conflict of interest."

"Oh, my. Whatever would give anyone that idea?"

"Mr. Gaunt!" the court cautions.

"Well, it wasn't how we saw it," Fitz-Niblick answers, clearly resigned now to the fact that it was all going to come out. "Not at all. It was just good business, especially for the Law Society."

"Do tell, Treasurer. Please, do tell."

"Your Honour," Mortimer objects. "This is his own witness he is browbeating. Why, I don't know, but there you are."

"I think it's pertinent," Her Honour rules, "and if you get impertinent again, Mr. Gaunt, I will remind you as well as the jury."

"Look," Fitz-Niblick answers, "there was nothing nefarious about it. Our idea was just this: Because we already knew how the operation worked, and because it was a Law Society operation, well, we, as benchers, should oversee it."

"A few select benchers."

"Benchers who had the ways and means to do it properly."

"And profit from it."

Fitz-Niblick laughs miserably. "Given that it was just about insolvent, profit wasn't on the immediate horizon, Mr. Gaunt."

"So you set up a company to deliberately lose money, including Mrs. Debeers' pension money?"

Fitz-Niblick struggles not to look exasperated, but he begins to flail. "No, no, not at all. We set the corporation up to get the thing, the hospitality division, back on the rails. Our thought was that we should bring better management in but maintain some sort of control over it, even though it was contracted out. Privatized, as you put it, Mr. Gaunt. We thought that was in the Law Society's interests."

"Sort of like John Beverley Robinson and his little land deal?"

"Let's not go there again, Mr. Gaunt," the judge rules off her own bat.

"You say, sir," Gaunt continues, "that your privatization scheme was in the Law Society's interests. Yet you didn't see fit to tell the rest of the benchers about it? And you were making it your own for-profit operation?"

"They knew about the scheme, but not the exact identity of all the players. That's all. We didn't want to get into a big debate before we had the details in place and we could explain it all lucidly."

"Before it was a *fait accompli*, you mean."

"Not at all. You might eat at Burger King every night. Maybe you even own shares in it. But you don't necessarily know who's running the everyday business, do you? You don't know where the meat and potatoes come from and who got them there. Why would you care?"

"Yet you went along with Debeers attacking the whole idea of privatization publicly, even though he was one of your partners in privatizing it."

"Again, Mr. Gaunt, I am not responsible for other people's views and public positions. I had no control over Jerry Debeers."

"You didn't? And what about the press, Treasurer? What were you doing about them? I mean Debeers had a lot of contact with them, didn't he?"

"Well, yes, there was Mr. Faddaster. He wasn't aware of exactly what we were doing, either, but he was nosing around, all right. Jerry was nervous about it, too." The treasurer chuckles, glancing again at the jury, working the crowd. "He's always nosing around, Mr. Faddaster is." The treasurer smiles, and about half the jury panel smiles back.

"You mean Dylan Faddaster, of the *Standard* newspaper."

"The very man."

"And what was the significance of that — of his nosing around?"

"Well, as I say, we wanted to avoid the wrong public relations angle on this, because then it would have destroyed the whole enterprise, all the careful planning and what-not, before it got off the ground. We didn't want to let the cat out of the bag, as it were."

Being only in the Treasurer's peripheral vision, and at shin level at that, I can't claim to have been the inspiration for this particular metaphor. But it strikes me as more than a little ironic. Apparently Gaunt feels the same way, or at least he has happened upon page 101 in *The Morris Dictionary of Word and Phrase Origins*, third shelf up, far left, north wall of Mr. Justice Mariner's chambers. He pauses, cocks that double-jointed mandible at the ceiling for a moment, glances with a little grin at Mortimer, then gazes with sincere bemusement on the witness, Samuel Fitz-Niblick, Q.C. "You know, Mr. Fitz-Niblick, speaking of pork-barrelling, I've read somewhere that the expression 'letting the cat out of the bag' is related to buying a 'pig in a poke.' At country fairs. Did you know that?"

"No, I didn't, sir. How interesting."

"Your Honour," Mortimer wearily hoists himself yet again. "Now we've moved from beans and the 1837 Rebellion to hog futures."

"At least we're moving, Mr. Mortimer."

"I'm just saying, Your Honour," Gaunt persists, "that apparently there were these fellows, con men, in fact, who plagued the country fairs in merrie olde England. Apparently they'd wander around with these sacks — pokes, they were called — with a wriggling animal inside. They'd find some credulous bumpkin and offer to sell him the nice, juicy suckling pig in the sack. And after the poor bumpkin paid his money and opened up his purchase, long after the seller had fled the scene, of course, the poor bumpkin, the buyer, he would find himself stuck with a mangy old stray cat."

Stuck. Mangy. Old. Charming.

"A pig in a poke," the judge muses, nodding. "When the cat's out of the bag."

"You've got it, Your Honour," Gaunt says.

The smile fades from the treasurer's face. Looking very grim, indeed, he tells Gaunt, "I'm simply saying, sir, that we didn't want Dylan Faddaster to give the public and the other benchers the wrong idea about our plans."

"What idea would that have been, then?"

"Your Honour," the treasurer pleads with the bench, "we've been over this."

"Please just answer, Mr. Fitz-Niblick."

"The wrong idea, Mr. Gaunt, was that we were lining our pockets." *Perish the thought,* I hissed, as did half the courtroom, it seemed, until the redoubtable Conchita called for order. "The same wrong idea you seem to be trying to give the jury."

"So what did you do to stop Mr. Faddaster from giving anyone this extraordinary idea — this idea you wanted to line your own pockets just because you'd run the catering into the ground and then used a secret corporation to buy it at a bargain basement price?" Gaunt speaks as fast as he can, nearly fainting, panting for breath by the end, but still careful to repeat the Treasurer's own damning words before the judge can cut him off.

Her Honour is not best pleased about this little gambit. She removes her designer spectacles and flings all eight-hundred dollars worth of them on her dais. "Mr. Gaunt, if you keep this up, we're going to have a very large problem on our hands with continuing this trial." She glowers at the jurors. "Members of the jury, there is not a scintilla of evidence that anyone ran the Law Society's dining services into the ground. Nor is there any evidence that anybody bought it for any price, let alone a bargain basement one."

"I'm sorry, Your Honour. Truly," Gaunt says, but he doesn't look it. And we all know how judges in criminal trials dislike offenders who fail to show remorse. Poor old Katrina. "Let me start again. Mr. Fitz-Niblick, as a business lawyer, you know something about buying and selling businesses, I take it."

"I hope so, Mr. Gaunt. And my clients hope so even more." The treasurer grins at the judge, who nods back.

"Isn't it true that, if you want to buy a business, you can get it a lot cheaper if it's all run down and losing money?"

"Sometimes. Sometimes not."

"But clearly it's worth more — and it costs more — if it's doing well."

"Generally speaking, yes. Of course."

"And if it's been mismanaged and you get it for a good price because of the bad management, well, if you manage it better, you can make a tidy profit from it, no?"

"Purely speculative, Your Honour," Mortimer objects. "If, if, if."

"And isn't it true, as well, that if the owners are fairly wealthy — like, business lawyers, for example — that if they're fairly wealthy, even if the business keeps losing money, well, they can get tax write-offs on the loss? And they can profit that way?"

"That's basic tax law, yes. But in this case, it's still speculative. Purely hypothetical."

"Okay." Gaunt shrugs. "Let me just ask this, then. Isn't it true that for various reasons, tax write-offs, trying to get around paying your ex-spouse a big fat divorce settlement, that sort of thing, isn't it true that people sometimes deliberately devalue their businesses? Understate the value, so that they don't have to pay big tax bills or divorce settlements, or whatever?"

"Mr. Gaunt," the judge interrupts. "I have no idea where you're going with this. You have zero proof that anyone's running anything down, and I'm instructing the jury again to remember that."

"Well, let me just ask Mr. Fitz-Niblick this, directly, as a business lawyer: If someone ruins a business that belongs to someone else, and then he wants to buy it for himself, doesn't that sort of smell, to put it politely, like a conflict of interest?"

"I didn't run anything into the ground, Mr. Gaunt. In fact, I've improved things, if you'll just look at the dining room these days. Anyway, my job, and a very difficult one it is, is to make sure the Law Society is managed in the best way possible for the profession as well as for the general public which it serves."

"If anyone's trying to place blame on you, sir, it's yourself. I was speaking in the general sense, hypothetically. And of course other people are involved here. Mr. Nobb. The deceased man, Mr. Debeers. Let's say somebody let the cat out of the bag and it became public that Jeremiah Debeers, self-appointed saint of the Law Society, wasn't so saintly after all."

"Well, that's what I mean about people misapprehending the facts. Jerry was very worried about that."

"I imagine so. He was quite religious, I understand."

"Quite."

"And he would have been pretty upset if people thought he was a false prophet, as it were."

The treasurer nods. "I think we can rest assured he would have been enraged."

"Okay, so let me put this to you again, Mr. Fitz-Niblick. What precisely did you do to stop Mr. Faddaster from blaming any of you very publicly — from giving others this unpleasant notion that you were false prophets who wanted to line your own pockets?"

"Well, Roman, Mr. Nobb, suggested that we make Mr. Faddaster an offer."

"How do you mean, an offer, Treasurer? An offer he couldn't refuse?" Gaunt essays a wicked little smile at the jury, but unfortunately it looks more like a dirty old man's leer.

"Well, bring him in, you know," Fitz-Niblick replies, "make him another shareholder in the corporation."

"How would you have done that?"

"I don't know. I suppose each of the other shareholders would have given him a share or so. Something like that. Issue more shares, maybe."

"Or maybe give him Ms. Slovenskaya's shares?"

"I have no idea, Mr. Gaunt. We hadn't got that far."

"And why was that?"

"Well, Jerry Debeers was quite opposed to bringing Dylan in. Incensed, in fact." The treasurer laughs quietly, now that the cat is out of the bag. "In fact, he kept calling us heretics — false prophets, I guess, Mr. Gaunt. He wanted it all top secret and he was afraid Dylan would give the game away. He said the fact that Dylan couldn't keep his mouth shut was why he normally went to him with confidential matters. It was quite ironic, really, when you think about it." The Treasurer chuckles at the jury, who stare impassively back at him until the smile fades from his lips. "And I think there might have been a little romantic rivalry there, too. Between Jerry and Dylan — regarding the fair Ms. Probert. Josey Probert, our fellow, or sister, bencher."

Gaunt and Mortimer exchange frank looks of surprise, then shrug at one another. Several jurors laugh.

At the same moment, Justice Mariner's secretary, Sandy Pargeter, enters, bows to the Bench, and brings a note to Leland Gaunt. Gaunt reads the document, then cocks his head at the ceiling, simultaneously shifting his jaw toward the floor. Finally, he asks the treasurer: "So you never made any offer at all to Mr. Faddaster? Never offered him some shares in the corporation, I mean?"

"No," the treasurer replies. "To this moment, so far as I know he has been unaware of our personal involvement."

"And will remain so, I am sorry to say, Your Honour." Gaunt turns suddenly, surprisingly, to the Bench. "For all eternity, it would seem. Your Honour, Mr. Faddaster was to be my next witness, but I have the sad duty to inform my friend Mr. Mortimer and this honourable court that Mr. Faddaster has passed away."

"You mean just now, Mr. Gaunt?" Justice M'Gonnigle asks, replacing her eyeglasses on her nose, abruptly leaning forward wide-eyed, her lips parted in a little o of surprise. "Suddenly?"

"Well, Your Honour, it's only just come to light, apparently. They only just discovered him. In his office, it seems."

"I see." Her Honour glances briefly at the jury and repeats, although she doesn't see anything, I don't imagine. "I see. Well, then, what would you like to do about that, Mr. Gaunt?"

"Perhaps this would be a good time for an adjournment, Your Honour. Just until tomorrow morning, so as not to inconvenience the jury?"

"Yes, perhaps it would be a good time to break off. Mr. Mortimer? Tomorrow morning at ten?"

"Of course, Your Honour. Of course. And I would like to express my condolences to Mr. Faddaster's family and colleagues."

"So would we all, Mr. Mortimer," Justice M'Gonnigle says. "So would we all."

CHAPTER 6

From Soup to Sanitation

I trot along behind the treasurer to his office, where Nobb is waiting at the door. "You heard the news, then?" Fitz-Niblick asks. "About Faddaster?" For some reason, probably unknown even to himself, he speaks in a hoarse whisper and looks furtively around him.

"Shocking," Nobb says in his normal voice, from his full, Parnassian height. "Shocking. He was a relatively young man, you know. Fat and dipsomaniacal, maybe . . ."

"But relatively young," Fitz-Niblick agrees, shaking his silver-pfitzered head in disbelief.

"Had a hell of a temper, too. Smoked like a chimney, on the quiet, I'm told. Almost burned down the whole *Standard* one night. All these papers and stuff he had piled everywhere. Fell asleep with a fag in his hand and set them alight."

"Smoked? What about the drinking? He was well pickled, that one. Permanently, I mean. I thought he would live forever, preserved in his own brine."

Nobb shakes his head sadly. "Wild man, he was."

"But relatively young."

"Let's call the paper, Sammy, shall we?"

"Right you are." Using the speakerphone, the treasurer gets Eustace Lacey, Faddaster's editor, on the line. Faddaster always liked to say that the *Standard* had brought Lacey in from London's *News of the World*, tabloid *ne plus ultra*, expressly to dumb down the Canadian daily. The official version of Lacey's mandate, though, was that his superiors expected him to get the paper "speaking the language of the ordinary taxpayer in the street." Faddaster had been one of Lacey's first hires.

"The long and short of it," Eustace Lacey tells the benchers, "is we just don't know how long the poor bugger'd been *hors de combat*."

"No," the treasurer says, winking at Nobb, then prodding at Yours Ear-Wiggingly with his hand-tooled Gucci kangaroo-hide loafer.

Although it wasn't unusual for Faddaster to sleep in his office, particularly when he'd been on a bender and it was too risky for him to drive home to the suburbs (he even kept a change of underwear stuffed behind the condom machine in the gents), he had been sick on and off for a few weeks, food poisoning or the stomach flu or something acutely gastrointestinal. "So everyone thought he was at home," Lacey explains. "Even the pong emanating from his office" — with walls not quite reaching the ceiling, apparently — "hadn't twigged anyone at first." Faddaster's office was always a sty, Lacey adds, with leftover take-out food, cola cans, dirty clothing, used handkerchiefs, and "you don't want to know what-all" strewn around, on the desk, the shelves, his computer monitor.

"And catch this. There were peanut shells everywhere, to boot." Lacey laughs. "It looked like one of those bars, you know, where you pitch 'em all over the floor on purpose. No kidding. I mean, the cleaners refused to darken the threshold. Your mate Debeers, just before he bought the farm, himself, he was bringing the nuts in for Faddaster by the lorry-load, fast as he could scarf 'em, in Tupperware containers, as fast as Dylan could suck 'em down. Loads of the stuff. Apparently Debeers got them from a client. Some snack foods supplier. Peanuts in the shell, and that other sort, too, you know, the fancier cocktail ones, roasted in oil. Faddaster squirreled those away for himself, went around everywhere with his greasy old pockets full of 'em. Shared the other ones around. Jesus. What a mess I'm in here, gents."

Lacey pauses, musing, apparently, about how selfish he sounds regarding his late, lamented front-line muckraker. "What a raver he was, eh, guys? Good newspaperman though, it must be said. He could be a pain in the arse, a splinter, just like your Debeers, I guess, but he got the job done. Sharpish, too. They were two of a kind, in their way, eh, gents?"

"The most painful way," Nobb mutters.

Newton's Third Law of Motion, I sagely add.

"Makes it all pretty ironic, I suppose," Lacey continues. "He'd give Debeers his 'empties,' the Tupperware, you know." He laughs. "Mrs. Debeers' Tupperware, for Chrissake, and Jerry'd go home or wherever and fill 'em up all over again. With bloody peanuts. Jesus. Peanuts!"

"Good morning, Treasurer Fitz-Niblick," Mortimer begins his cross-examination, rather more cordially than defence counsel, the skinny little nebbish-nobody law clerk who had called the elegant Queen's Counsel as his own witness.

"Good day to you, Mr. Mortimer," Fitz-Niblick replies, smiling, looking all refreshed and newly confident.

"This won't take long, sir. Can you tell us where you were on the evening of Sunday, the eighth of June of last year?"

"Well, from four until about dinnertime, I was in a meeting of the Hospitality Committee. I am co-chair, or, chair, now, I suppose. Mr. Debeers was the other co-chair, you see."

"And you were in that meeting until what time?"

"Oh, it must have been six-thirty or so. Some of the members stayed behind for a chat, and then I worked in my office for a while."

"And you remember that how?"

"Well, I'm told it's the day Jerry died. So we've all had occasion to think about it quite a bit."

"And did Jerry Debeers stay behind at that meeting?"

"I don't believe so, no. He had a dinner engagement or something of the sort. With our colleague Josey Probert, I think it was."

"And normally you wouldn't have expected Jerry to be there on a Sunday?"

"That's right. For religious or family reasons, he generally did not attend the Sunday meetings."

"So you and the others in the meeting had no reason to think he'd be there that day?"

"Well, based on past Sunday meetings, no."

"And you weren't in the library at all that day? The Great Library?"

"No, sir. Not at all. The rest of the time, it being Sunday, well,

I was at home with my own family, of course."

"Of course, sir. And this corporation, the one you hoped would take over the hospitality operations. Whose idea was that?"

"Well, I guess Roman and I both sort of thought it up, in our work as benchers. As I say, it was a way of maintaining management within the Law Society, and we thought it would make Jerry more amenable to the whole idea of privatization. If we showed him we could maintain control, I mean. And sure enough, he bought in. I mean, he accepted the idea in principle. Faster than we'd thought, in fact."

"So he was against it, but you persuaded him over to your view."

"Well, I suppose we helped him to see the other side. Yes."

"So the principal motive behind your company was not in fact personal gain?"

The treasurer laughs. "Again, the thing was losing money at the time, Mr. Mortimer. The motives were to placate Jerry and keep some management control while we got the thing off the Law Society's books and into the hands of professionals. We're lawyers, Mr. Mortimer, not chefs or restaurateurs. It was simply a management thing. A delegation of function, if you will."

"And in the time since Mr. Debeers' death, the dining room is in fact doing rather better, isn't it?"

To demonstrate equivocation, or perhaps theatrical modesty, the treasurer bobbles his head. "Well, I'd like to think my little improvements will show some effects over time, Mr. Mortimer." He smiles self-effacingly. "But it's early days, yet. Early days." He sighs. "Only time will tell." He shrugs.

Mortimer sits down as the jury chuckles, perhaps in relief more than politeness, given that (speaking of dining) lunch was on the horizon.

You could call it my contribution to the paper, I suppose, salient, provocative, even, carefully deposited just after the third paragraph on page thirty-eight of "Environmentalist Protesters and the *Public Lands Act*: Reasonable Limits on the 'Reasonable Limits' We Impose on Free Expression and Mobility Rights." I mean, we were supposed to be endorsing *free expression* here, no?, preserving nature's forests, not pandering to privately held forestry interests? Have a read of *this* folderol: *No organized protests without government licences. Laws that make the protesters pay personally for any damage they do to real property, equipment, logging roads, or logging rights. Stiffer penalties for failure to obey court orders to stay off the logging sites and for other contempts.*

Yes, on peer review, the less imaginative might see my contribution as nothing other than a slimy hairball, garnished for that environmentalist flavour with a few leaves of grass, half a housefly, and that insipid kibble His Lordship buys on special offer, incontrovertible evidence of yet another breach of probation, taking me yet another step closer to Her Majesty's Doghouse on River Street. And now that I mention it, that could well prove to be His Lordship's point of view. *Take him down, bailiff.* He's been manifestly grumpy lately about this free expression lark.

And of course there is that famous rift between law and justice. Take the old saw, for example, that every dog is allowed one bite. It is doubtful that this was ever a genuine principle of law. I can tell you for sure that there has never existed any general principle allowing the resident cat one pardoned scratching incident on John Beverley Robinson's armchair, or a single get-out-of-jail-free urine shower on the newel post and red carpet in the front foyer, just under the portrait of Sir William Osgoode. Humans have regarded cats now and then as being just as verminous as the Black Death rats they control. Dogs never have suffered such defamation.

Then again, history repeatedly recognizes that cats have their uses in Has-beings culture. It is well known that the ancient Egyptians worshipped cats. Their law prescribed capital punishment for sylvestricide.

In 936, the Welsh king Howell the Good proclaimed a law that a cat should be "perfect of ear, perfect of eye, perfect of teeth, perfect of claw, and without marks of fire" — meaning the hearthfire. A newborn kitten was statutorily valued at a penny. From the time it opened its eyes to when it could hunt vermin it was valued at two pence, and when it was of ripe hunting age it could fetch four pence.

If you killed a Welshman's cat, you were indebted to him for a quantity of threshed wheat equal in depth to the distance between the cat's nose and tail tip when the feline was held by the tail, perpendicular to the ground. In other words, damages took account of the lost value of the animal as a pest-control service. Apparently there was no discount if the owner acquired a replacement cat. The offence was too serious to attract mitigation.

Yes, Grimalkin's namesake probably suffered terribly at the hands of the law, cats being guilty by association with witches. *Double, double, toil and trouble.* We shared the blame of other outcasts for the Plague, which defamation probably prolonged the epidemic. Rousting, torturing, and murdering cats wouldn't have gone very far in reducing the rat population of England and the Continent.

Times improved again for *felis sylvestris* when insurance companies refused to issue policies on grain consignments unless ships carried a proper mouser. Evidently a ship's captain could be personally liable in negligence if anything happened to the seafaring moggy. And then there's the cat as revolutionary. At least one aristocrat escaped starvation in the Tower of London when his cat, incarcerated with him, climbed the Tower chimney to bring back a freshly killed pigeon.

The law, in other words, has traditionally respected the cat's economic importance — importance to the economy of nature as well as in human commerce. And indeed there is one documented instance where the law excused a cat attack because it was a first offence. The cat, in other words, was allowed something like one bite. I have heard Justice Mariner tell the story himself on several occasions, describing it as a well-known case among British barristers.

It seems that a witness in a county court matter was unhappy about the proceedings. The story goes that she pulled a dead cat from a paper bag and hurled it at the judge. Apparently the cat hit the dais or fell harmlessly to the floor. The judge considered the evidence there, then informed the witness: "Madam, if you do that again, I shall commit you for contempt of court."

It will not have been obvious to the jury, or anyone else, that Gaunt's next witness, Murray "Moishe" Feldman, is a multi-millionaire entrepreneur. With his bush of curly silver hair, thickly black-rimmed glasses, oily skin and bulbous red nose, my old landlord and patron looks astonishingly like Jerry Garcia, the late guitarist and putative singer for the Grateful Dead. Moishe seems pleased enough to perform, too, although he keeps blinking and swallowing extravagantly — nictitating describes it better, I suppose, given that it is more a convulsion than a flickering of the eyelids and the wetting of his whistle. Happily, Feldman is here merely and briefly to explain his business dealings with Jerry Debeers.

"How did you get to know Mr. Debeers?" Gaunt asks him.

"He used to come into my restaurant in the old days. When my partner and I first got going at our little deli in Kensington Market, Tokyo Moishe's Oriental Deli and Catering, it was called. And then we got reacquainted when he was acting for a buyer on some condominium sales. I was the seller." *Nictitation.* "As well as the developer. Of the condo building, I mean."

"And did you have any dealings with Jerry Debeers subsequently?"

"Yes. We became friends, and" *nictitation* "also I became a regular client of Jerry's."

"How so?"

"He acted as my lawyer on some of my real estate transactions. I expanded out of the restaurant business into real property development. And then we, Jerry and I, became partners."

"Partners how?"

"Well, in some of the real estate development. And also in the catering supply business."

"Tell us about the catering supply."

"Oh, we were just beginning to build it, I guess. It was snack foods, mostly. Packaged sandwiches. Candy bars. Chips, nuts, juice, pop, that sort of thing. Party snacks. And in the last few months we were expanding into actual cocktail party goodies. That was Jerry's idea. A little upscale. Canapés and such. It was new for me, and I like a challenge. We'd applied for a licence as liquor brokers, too."

"Who were your clients?"

"Oh, Jerry's church. Some of our own buildings, with the vending machines and such. That was what motivated us to start the venture, really. We sold little boxes of detergents and softener for the laundry rooms, too. And there were the schools where some of Jerry's church friends sent their kids. That sort of thing. He was well connected, on the sly. He was a good businessman, Jerry, on the sly."

"So I understand. Any other clients of interest?"

"Well, the Law Society, of course."

"So Jerry was partners with you in a business that was already supplying the Law Society?"

"Oh, yeah. For the past year or so, I'd say."

"And did you have any other business with the Law Society?"

"Well, I was hoping to. Jerry and I were putting in a bid to run the catering there. The dining room and all that. Jerry was trying to get it privatized."

"On the sly."

"Well, I don't know, really . . ."

"So you and he would have been supplying your own catering service at the Law Society. If he got it privatized?"

"Well, that was the plan. Sort of like McDonald's raising its own cows and selling itself its own beef. If you're your own supplier, well, it's easier to keep your costs down and your profits up.

And we hoped eventually to buy out the other partners in the catering service. So we'd be running the whole thing on our own — from soup to sanitation, as we liked to say."

"I see. And were the other benchers aware that you were already supplying food to the Law Society, even before privatization?"

"I couldn't tell you for sure, but I wouldn't have thought so. As far as I know, they had no reason to wonder who the shareholders were in our catering company. And it had no name — it was just a numbered company."

"So it was anonymous."

"Pretty much, yeah. Anyway, it was just business, and they had no reason to wonder who the shareholders were, any more than I know who holds the majority shares in Burger King or, you know, McDonald's."

I wonder where we've heard that before.

"I wonder where we've heard that before," Gaunt picks up the cue.

"Let's save the commentary for your closing, Mr. Gaunt," Justice M'Gonnigle says.

"But some of the benchers might have known?"

"Maybe, but as I say, we — I mean Jerry and me — we weren't involved in the daily operations," Moishe Feldman continues. "Our staff dealt with the kitchen people — the hospitality manager, mostly, and the maître-d', Jean-Pierre — not with the benchers."

"And was Jerry listed on the corporate documents? Of that first catering company, I mean?"

"Oh, no. His mother was a director, and so was my wife. Jerry and I were just ordinary shareholders."

"Why was that?"

"Well, for the usual reasons. Extra protection from creditors and that sort of thing. Extra protection from personal liability."

"A way of keeping your involvement, and Jerry's involvement, secret? In a numbered company?"

"You could put it like that." *Nictitation.* "But it's a commonly accepted business practice. It's done every day." *Nictitation.* "Legally."

"So we've heard, Mr. Feldman," Justice M'Gonnigle says, blinking and stretching her neck as though the witness's tics are contagious. "So we've heard."

CHAPTER 7

Verdict

"Your Honour," Gaunt begins the afternoon's evidence, "the defence calls Ms. Katrina Daniella Slovenskaya."

The guard sitting next to the dock opens its side door and the star of the drama emerges from her cage. It is a vaguely thrilling moment, a figurative sort of casting down the shackles — casting them down, but on the ecstatically dreadful chance that the prisoner's freedom will prove horribly brief. The experience is a reminder, really, a taste of what it was like the day before the terror began, but with the certain knowledge that darkness will fall and the nightmare will recur, that it was merely hiding from the light, like a vampire. Over time, after all, the prisoner's dock earns its comforts as a sort of home away from home, a gated community of one, safe as a kitty carry-case. One would rather give her evidence from there, perhaps, where she has got used to the surroundings, however stained and miserable. Still, Katrina re-emerges into the waking world, blinking, short and plump, loping a little, toward the witness box, her face and forehead a riot of rosacial splotches as she stares fearfully at the floor, wisps of hair cascading from her grandmotherly bun, ill at ease as the centre of attention at any time, never mind when she is charged with committing murder with malice aforethought and upon pain of life imprisonment.

She looks up at her lawyer, her forehead deeply creased, her lips a thin white line.

Did she know the nature of the corporation of which she was a director?

Well, Jerry had explained it as a real estate development and investment vehicle. A nest egg, for her retirement. For her, he said, it would be like having a totally secure mutual fund without the management fees. For her retirement. And she believed it. He was a good man. A devout Christian man.

Was he now? And how did she know that?

After he became a bencher, he was a familiar face at the library. He seemed to make a point of coming into the Reference Room to chat with her colleague, Elise Throckmorton. He had a bit of a crush on Elise, it seemed. A lot of the lawyers did. Elise had that waifish, delicate look which attracted men; the wan smile, the deferential turning away of her head with its honey-toned, silky hair. She looked delicate, in need of protection, although really she was made of sterner stuff than potato-patch Katrina. Anyway, she, Katrina, got to know Jerry that way, because her desk was right next to Elise's. And because he was polite and friendly and thoughtful, well, he talked to her, too, included her in their chats. And he discovered that she was a Christian, or at least a regular church-goer. They were like-minded to that extent.

Was she jealous of the attention he paid Elise?

A little, yes. But she knew that Elise was not really interested in Jerry. There was Jake, Elise's husband. And they had two kids. And Jerry was a good Christian man.

And as far as she knew he was really against privatizing the food and hospitality services at Osgoode Hall?

He was totally against it. Until the day he died. Absolutely.

Ah. And now that she mentioned it, would she tell the jury what she knew about that? About the day Jerry Debeers died.

There is a very long silence. Then, Katrina Slovenskaya slowly bows her head, trembles, and begins to weep. She shudders with grief. The jury watches for a moment, then inspects its hands, looks up in the air, off to the side, not at Katrina, not at the judge (who herself stares hard and deliberately at nothing in particular), but at the dais between them. Outside, Ernie the Evangelist is preaching:

For I have heard a voice as of a woman in travail, and the anguish. Woe is me now! For my soul is wearied because of murderers.

Katrina raises her head, her face wet and blurred, her babushka doll features almost washed away in her desolation, her mouth gaping and ugly with a *cri de coeur*, a howl from the very bottom of that Hell every creature will visit at one time or another in its life on this earth.

The voice of the daughter of Zion. It is a condition of life on Earth that we gaze at some time or other into its black and airless core and hear nothing but our own cries echoing back at us. *I am a superstitious atheist.*

Katrina's eyes widen as she squints at these notions in the fetid darkness. And then she says: "I killed him." She weeps again, but with the relief of confession, bowing. *You live alone.*

The anguish of her that bringeth forth her first child. That bewaileth herself, that spreadeth her hands, saying, Woe is me now!

"I killed him."

Tell us how, Katrina. Slowly. It's all right now. The worst is over. Just tell us how.

"He told me there was something wrong with the photocopier and Josey wanted to use it after hours. She was going to photocopy something while we went out to dinner together, Jerry and I. I was flattered. I liked him. Dinner. . . . Anyway, he was going to repair the plug first, he said, so Josey wouldn't have the same trouble he'd been experiencing with it. He'd brought his little tool kit, the one he used at home when he worked on his model trains."

The witness smiles, fluttering her eyelids up at her lawyer.

"He had quite a nifty little layout down there in his basement. He was so proud of it. The trains, I mean. He'd driven me over to the house to show them to me, when we were setting up the corporation. Around the time he wanted me to invest in the company, I mean, and be a director. He was courting me, but just for that, of course. So he took me over to his house to show me the trains."

Katrina laughs softly, looking directly now at Leland Gaunt.

"He must have known I would see through him. Did he think I was stupid?

"Anyway, he was like a little boy with those model trains. He specialized in the old Lionel model railways, you know, because the British ones, they were harder to come by, he said, expensive. But his were still worth quite a bit, apparently. He was so proud of them. Anyway . . ."

Anyway, she went downstairs to the first floor with Jerry because she was supposed to turn off the power to the Journals Room, so he could test the photocopier plug after he'd fixed it. She helped him pull the copier away from the wall a little, so he could get at the plug. Otherwise, you had to jam your hand in there, because of the column wall where the outlet was located. And then she went off toward the utility room downstairs, to switch off the power. Only it turned out that Josey was already in the library. Apparently she had come in during the afternoon to do some work in the Reading Room. And at that point, Josey had decided to get on with her photocopying. She said Jerry had told her to use the photocopier in the Journals Room because it was more private and less used — more likely to have a good supply of paper and toner. So Josey and Katrina got to chatting, there in the stairway corridor outside the Journals Room where Jerry was working on the photocopier. They lost track of time until they heard the popping noises.

What was that? Josey asked. I said it was probably nothing. The old building and old books are always making complaint, I said. Like grumpy old men, the ghosts of all those old men whose portraits hang in the library, and all around Osgoode Hall. It's haunted by angry, disappointed, self-righteous white men. Dead white men. If these walls could talk, I said, they would piss and moan.

"You see, Jerry didn't want her to know that he was working on the machine. Only the service people were supposed to touch it, really, but Jerry said why should we draw down on the credit we had on our service contract when he could easily fix it. He was always looking to economize like that. His election platform was lower fees, less expense. For the members, that is. He was proud of that, and he always said actions spoke louder than words. He was a little pedantic that way. It was his duty as a budget-conscious bencher and all that, he said. He didn't want to be a false prophet, he said, and God helped those who helped themselves. He had the tools, he said. It was just a plug. You didn't need an expert for a little plug. So I told Josey it was probably nothing. But then we heard another noise, the popping sound, I mean, but more like a little explosion that time, and Josey went rushing off toward the Journals Room. I came in just behind her. And we found him. Poor Jerry, I mean."

"So, you see, I killed him. It was my fault. He did whatever splicing or whatever he was going to do. And he must have thought that by then I'd turned the power off. But I was waylaid . . . distracted. We got to talking, Josey and I. And so then I guess he plugged the thing back in, but the power was still on and whatever he did only made the plug more dangerous. So, yes, I killed him.

"That's what it felt like, and in the heat of the moment Josey and I panicked, as she testified. We decided that it was better for everyone if we just left and maybe phoned in an anonymous 9-1-1 or something like that. So we pushed the photocopier back against the wall, with poor Jerry just lying against it, and I collected all the tools in their little Tupperware box. Because we thought we might get found out, you see, if it was obvious what Jerry was doing there. I mean, here I gave him after-hours access and he electrocutes himself while I'm letting him work on the photocopier, which he's not supposed to do in the first place. I live with my sister, you see. Otherwise, I'm alone. Totally alone. No other family or whatever. A spinster, they used to say. As Mr. Mortimer said. I need my job, Mr. Gaunt. I'm just a few years away from retirement. I can't afford to lose my job. I just can't. And now, even my investment in the company is gone. . . .

"So then we went for tea, as Josey said, and we decided not to tempt fate. Poor Jerry was dead. We couldn't change that. Nobody could. And it would have been really bad if it looked like we were somehow mixed up in it. Suspicious. He was already gone, and there was nothing we could do. So we decided it was better if we just left him. You know. There."

Katrina breaks down again, poor soul, and looks like she would will herself dead, too, were she able, another homicide on her hands to expiate the one she blames on herself.

"For someone else to find. Whether we reported it or somebody else found him, it didn't matter at that point. Poor, poor Jerry."

She had lied about one thing before, though, hadn't she?

"No, sir. I've told the whole truth. As painful as it is. Everything."

But wasn't it true that she was in love with Jerry Debeers? Wasn't that the whole truth?

Katrina breaks down again, and we watch for several excruciating moments until Leland Gaunt says at last: "Those are my questions, Your Honour."

Well, of course Mortimer does the decent thing. He's not a bad lot; in prosecuting, he's just putting the state's case, after all. That is his job, and his necessary function in what you Has-beings like to call the administration of justice, which itself, of course, is largely a mythical construct. *I can't forgive God for not existing. Law is not justice.* The Crown is said to be neutral as between Her Majesty and her subjects. That's the line they take at the Attorney

General's, anyway. Glancing sympathetically at the accused, Madam Justice M'Gonnigle directs the jury to acquit Katrina Slovenskaya and we — Justice Mariner, Leland Gaunt, Gordie Mortimer, and Yours Newly Confident in the Presumption of Innocence — adjourn to the Gentlemen Barristers' Robing Room for our own post-mortem.

"Holy fucking doodle, boys!" Mortimer says. "I guess the jolt was meant for poor old Josey Probert, then. Who'd'a thunk it? Holy fucking doodle."

"Looks like it, Gordie," Justice Mariner replies. "We'll never know for sure, of course, but that's what it would appear."

"What?" Gaunt asks, looking baffled, never mind that he's just pulled off the victory of his career. *Not guilty of first-degree murder.* "You think Debeers meant to do his best friend in?"

Mortimer laughs and shakes his head. "Lee! You mean you dragged the courtroom floor with my case and you didn't even know what you were doing? Give me strength!"

"Well, Lee," His Lordship says, shrugging at his ingenuous clerk, "she just about had the goods on him, didn't she? All she had to do was put her head together with Faddaster's — and I gather the old pillow talk was possible there, if difficult to imagine."

Spare us, please.

"And as Fitz-Niblick said," Mortimer adds, "there might have been some sexual jealousy around that business as well. Between Debeers and Faddaster, I mean, over the unaccountably attractive Ms. Probert."

"Well, Gordie, there's no accounting for taste," Justice Mariner says, shrugging. "I mean, Probert and *Faddaster*? And he was a pretty repressed guy, Debeers. Wouldn't you say?"

Action, opposite and equal reaction, I add, threading back and
forth among their six legs.

"Just waiting to blow a gasket."

"Blow something," Mortimer says. "They get to comparing
notes, Faddaster and Probert, or she starts to put two and two
together on her lonesome, and the party's over for old Jerry and
his Establishment cronies. Not so holier than thou after all. Family
Compact of the new millennium. Let's run the Hall for our own
benefit. Let's get rich off the kitty. Personally speaking, my Law
Society fees are already high enough, thank you kindly, even if Her
Majesty pays them at present."

The Has-beings are briefly silent as Mortimer stuffs his gown
into its blue bag. Then he says: "I guess he figured she'd just reach
for the plug without looking."

"Well you would, wouldn't you?" Justice Mariner asks. "If the
thing's jammed against the wall like that, well, you'd just reach
behind it and feel around for the plug. And I guess the foil helped
get the current going between the exposed wires. He'd cut the
ground wire, too. . . . Debeers was just enough of an electrician to
do it fairly quickly, I guess. Otherwise, it didn't take any particular expertise, did it?"

"That reminds me, Gaunt," Mortimer says, turning to His
Lordship's clerk. "This is not really continuing disclosure, exactly,
but you might like to know that while you were with the press out
there, hugging and mugging with your client after the acquittal,
the cops called me on the cell phone. While I was having a smoke
outside."

Yes, his dirty old gown fairly reeks of it.

"The old lady, Jerry's mom, she had them back at her place this morning. Apparently this year's Beaujolais Nouveau had just flooded her basement." Mortimer laughs, but sadly, shaking his head again. "And now they think Jerry might have been involved in Faddaster's death, too."

Poor Leland Gaunt is not the only one present who is suddenly and totally dumbfounded. With his tee-shirt half over his head, he honks through an armhole as His Lordship shrugs and asks: "What in God's name *are* you talking about, Gordie?"

Basements. A natural habitat for your *felis sylvestris*, of course. Yes, I know the one at Osgoode well. As you might expect, most pretence is abandoned there. The concrete walls of the narrow corridors are painted an industrial straw blonde, like the walls of the notorious wine cellar and the pipes and other guts of the pretty beast, complete with valve wheels to adjust steam and ventilation levels. Had I the strength, it would be hard to resist giving them a twirl or two, just to satisfy my curiosity. There are the barracks-style lavatories, their stalls divided by thick slabs of construction grade marble on which generations of students have recorded critiques of the bar admission course amid the more mundane scatologica. The printing and electrical plants are down there, as well, and the staff cafeteria where they run the Out of the Cold soup kitchen. But coldness prevails. Concrete, galvanized iron, featureless linoleum.

Presumably the basement *chez* Debeers is somewhat more homey. From what I hear, it is certainly warm, and on the occasion in question, not a little redolent of wine vinegar. The scene when the police arrived, as I understand it, appeared something like this:

"I'm hearing explodings," Anika Debeers tells the wide-eyed constables. She's all flushed and breathless, mopping her brow with a kitchen towel. "I don't know what. I'm looking. Is all on floor. I'm thinking, what is? We don't got wine in this my house. Never."

"Well, ma'am," Police Constable Plod says. "It's a little hot down here, don't you think, for storing wine? I mean, from what I understand, you're not to store it in conditions over fifty or sixty degrees Fahrenheit. Something like that."

Mrs. Debeers shakes her head resolutely, pulling her cardigan around her sinewy frame. "I no like cold. Anyways, sir, I no store no wine in. Please. No."

It arose, of course, that some of the labels — including that of a $349 Meursault and a $625 St. Émilion — matched those unaccounted for in the Law Society log. Presumably the Splinter intended to sell the Law Society's wine right back to it, through the corporation he ran with Moishe Feldman. Or maybe he just wanted to make the other benchers think the place was so badly run, it needed better management to stop all the filching — it needed privatization, as Leland Gaunt had said in court. And if Debeers could discredit some of his fellow shareholders at the same time, all the better for buying them out at a fire-sale price. No doubt to his self-righteous mind this subterfuge was nothing like theft, his Law Society fees and labour as a bencher having been used to purchase the demon's brew he never shared. He was just taking his fair portion, and working in the greater public interest, doing Good Works. Religion, or superstition (choose your poison), has its own logic. While P.C. Plod tiptoes through the pungent mess, his colleague, Constable Babyface, can't resist playing with the model trains, now of the estate of Jeremiah Debeers. A derailment ensues, and one of the little freight cars marked Canadian National dumps its greasy cargo all over the little tracks and plywood underneath, painted to look like the countryside of the pre-Cambrian shield in north-central North America.

"Peanuts!" Constable Babyface says, popping one into his mouth, only to spit it out, just as expeditiously. "*Mouldy* peanuts!" All the little freight cars contain them, it turns out. Virginia cocktail peanuts circling round and round, a cross-basement trek going nowhere in the dank air.

"I mean," Mortimer says, back with us in the robing room at the University courthouse, "it would tie up everything with a cute little bow to say that our two dead guys were hoist on their own petards. Wouldn't it? And maybe they were. But even if Debeers was turning Faddaster's mouldy peanut scheme back on him. . . ."

"To get him out of the picture, you mean, like Josey," Gaunt says, "to protect the corporation and the privatization scheme?"

"Yeah, to get him and Probert both out of the picture, for whatever reason. But even if we can assume that's what he was up to, the cops' pathologist says it was longer than a long shot. The stuff, the peanut mould — aflatoxin, it's called — it can cause acute liver failure, apparently, but it would have to have been pretty damn concentrated. Debeers' method was just too primitive to deliver a killer dose by itself."

"So it's the double murder that wasn't."

"Well. I think Debeers would have seen it as a holy war. Regime change. Good triumphs over evil. Moral strength over carnal weakness. All's fair in love and Crusade."

"It's pretty academic now, anyway, I guess." His Lordship shrugs. "Still, you were right about one thing, Gordie. It was all about love and money."

Mortimer, however, is still on the peanuts. "The nuts made the poor bastard pretty damn sick, though, apparently," he says. "Damn sick. And seeing how he already had advanced cirrhosis, diabetes, heart trouble, and I don't know what-all, well, it might have pushed him right over the edge. That's what the forensic guys are saying. Might have been the last straw — or legume."

"Like Jerry Debeers and his cardiac," Justice Mariner adds. "And all for nothing. The whole privatization scheme's blown out of the water anyway, now."

"Well, I don't know about that, Judge." Mortimer shakes his head. "But Fitz-Niblick and Nobb can kiss their investment in it goodbye. You can take that one to the bank."

"Or not," His Honour replies. "You see it from the bench all the time. Some of these folks have a way of rising back up good as new, Gordie, out of their own ashes. Or noxious mould, as it were."

PART THREE

In Mercy

Closing Argument

A closing argument for *felis sylvestris* and all those like us, we quiet ones who shrink wilfully into the shadows:

By your leave. Are we, as it is often said, aloof? Disinterested? Self-involved?

Not guilty.

Are we self-conscious?

Absolutely. For our pride rests uneasily on the knowledge that we are always at your mercy.

This is the argument I make, mutely of course, to His Lordship, in mitigation of sentence for my various and sundry breaches of the rule of law over the last eighteen or twenty months here at Osgoode Hall. *By your leave. Forgive me, Lord, for I have sinned.* All in all, however, have I not been in the Hall's vanguard for the administration of justice — constantly multi-tasking, to adopt the contemporary Has-being argot, as consultant on "Environmentalist Protesters and the Public Lands Act," extermination of sundry vermin within and without Osgoode Hall, the blossoming of Leland Gaunt, Esq., the dethroning of corrupt benchers, not to mention murder most "fowl," or at least death by one's own petard?

By your leave, My Lord. I am at your mercy. Let me stay. My Lord. Let me stay. By your leave. I beg your pardon.

Are we not much alike, My Lord, the perfect companions? Like you, I detest being lonely, but I often prefer to be left alone.

Oh, but of course, never mind, sorry to trouble you just now. My petition and your decision can await yet another day. *Sine die*, as we put it at the Court of Appeal: without a fixed day. When we get to it. Of course. *I beg your pardon.* Works for me, My Lord. Naturally. *Felis sylvestris* doesn't mind being kept in suspense. The cat's life is always *sine die*, and not only because we are nocturnal. We live that we live — without day, never knowing what comes next, but anticipating it all the same. You might say that suspense is the story of our life. It is how we conduct ourselves, always on the lookout. Cautious, if not suspicious. Q.C.: Questing Cats. In mercy, as I say. Without day. Begging your pardon. For I see that you are distracted by something more pressing. The mail has arrived. *In mercy.*

The Honourable Theodore E. Mariner
The Ontario Court of Appeal
Osgoode Hall
Toronto, Ontario

Dear Mr. Justice Mariner:
Re: Conference papers, Tenth Annual ICE
in Paris, France
We regret to inform you that we cannot at last accept

your paper, "Environmentalist Protesters and the Public Lands Act: Reasonable Limits on 'the Reasonable Limits' We Impose on Free Expression and Mobility Rights," for publication in the conference papers of The Tenth Annual International Conference on Environmental Law (ICE). As you will recall, our original commission to you required that, for the purposes of the polemical discussion, you would adopt the so-called "Save the Forests" position, in favour of the free expression in all cases of protest excepting the most extreme variety, such as where the protesters are endangering the human life or otherwise resorting to the physical violence. Upon reviewing your paper most recently, the Publications Review Committee have found that you instead have present the so-called logging case, namely, the arguments for limiting the free expression so as to ensure that the environmentalism does not unduly interfere with the economic efficiencies in the natural resources sector of the internationalist markets. As we understand your thesis, you are arguing that the global economic and related rights should take precedence over the majority of the environmentalist positions.

Unfortunately, this does not conform with our original commission as agreed with you. Please note that we do not take this position arbitrarily. Our problem is that we already are feature three excellent presenters who are taking for us the so-called prior restraint view, the position, that is, that restraining the free expression among environmentalists and the anti-globalization activists amounts to "such limits as are demonstrably justified in a free and democratic society," to adopt the words of your Canadian Charter of Rights and Freedoms. As you will appreciate, another such paper, one such as yours, would serve to unbalance the panel as we have carefully constructed it. As well, we had hoped that a representative from your Canada, which depends so heavily on the lumber and pulp and paper industries, could bring to us a particular insight on balancing the economic interests against the urgings of the liberal humanism. Therefore, we have invited Madam Justice Farbiss-Noor, your sister judge from the British Columbia Court of Appeal, to substitute for you on the panel. We are given to understand that it is in that province, in fact, where much of the Canadian forestry industry is based. You will agree we are sure that this makes Justice Farbiss-Noor a valuable addition to the panel, and we most optimistically look forward to a lively debate on the issue at the Tenth International.

Please feel free, however, to join us at the Presenters' Cocktail Meet-and-Greet the evening before the conference begins.

Yours sincerely,

Hans-Joachim Dorfmann
Co-ordinator, Tenth ICE
Hamburg, GDR

After reading the letter from Herr Dorfmann, I move to the window to survey my kingdom where I mete and dole unequal laws unto a savage race: Osgoode Hall in autumn. Its autumn and mine,

I suppose. There is widespread agreement that fall would be the city's loveliest season were it not harsh winter's *entré*. Amid the orange and red leaves, and the last blooms of the asters and geraniums, the grounds crew is hard at their fall clean-up. Even through the double glazing in Justice Mariner's chambers, the sharpened and vibrating air is pungent with the spent fuel of chainsaws as the crew removes the young apricot trees from their small copse near the walkway to Queen Street West. The workers have driven their little truck onto the dying lawn nearby, the vehicle's bed loaded with stones (some of them nearly boulders), bulbs, tubers, and tiny bedding plants — creeping thyme, woolly thyme, dianthus, alyssum, hens and chickens, lobelia, northern cacti . . . hardy perennials, like Yours Enduringly. Somewhere else, in the cab perhaps, or under the burlap and top soil heaped near the stones, there is a metal spike mounted with a brass plaque. A couple of weeks ago, and under my careful supervision, His Lordship prepared its copy:

Glacial Rock Garden gift of
the Honourable Justice Theodore E. Mariner,
of the Ontario Court of Appeal,
on the inauguration of
the 'Landscape Legacy' Program
established by the Benchers of
the Law Society of Upper Canada.
Erected this 24th day of October . . .

One by one, the workers uproot the young apricot trees and pile their remains next to the truck. So begins the long anticipation of another spring. On appeal. Without day. In mercy.

Can't wait for more Amicus, Q.C. (Questing Cat)?
Here's a sneak preview of his next novel-length adventure,
Murder's Out of Tune, by Jeffrey Miller, coming Spring, 2005.

PART ONE

Til Death Us Do Part

CHAPTER 1

Overture:
Things Ain't What They Used to Be

How Many of You Are There in the Quartet? That was the title of a book Des Cheshire kept threatening to write. He got the idea, he said, from the question airline attendants frequently asked him as he travelled with Billy Wonder from gig to gig around the world: "And how many of you are there in the quartet?" But now it was no joke. Suddenly, the answer was three — now that Billy Wonder sat slumping sideways against the piano's soundboard, with two drumsticks hanging off the piano wire twisted around his neck.

In twenty-two years of touring, their show had never opened quite like this. Tommy Profitt, the comic, had warmed up the crowd as he normally did when he wasn't too juiced to go on. As usual, he had performed in front of the curtain on the bandstand, perched on a stool, brandishing the morning's newspaper. When Tommy finished his angry intellectual act, Jersey Doucette shook his head in practiced disgust, looking like he could just about keep himself from spitting on his own floor, and picked up the microphone he kept behind his bar. He snapped the mic on with a loud pop, breathed sonorously into the sound system, then mumbled in his wet and gravelly *basso profundo*, "And now, ladies and gentlemen, in their exclusive two-week run at the Chicken Alley in the heart of Yorkville, a warm welcome, please, for our feature attraction, the Billy Wonder Quartet."

It was like the voice of God, but on codeine.

Popping the mic off, Jersey pressed the doorbell switch mounted under the bar's ledge and the motor on the automatic curtain stuttered into action like a used-up electric cake-mixer. Briefly. As usual, Jersey had to hike over to the stage and give the mechanism a manual assist, getting a bigger laugh from the packed club than Tommy had managed during his entire routine. Jersey pulled the curtain wide to reveal Billy spot-lit at the piano. The rest of the stand was dark, but if you squinted you could just make out in silhouette Jimmy Whitehead at his bass, Terry Denver on drums, and Des — aloof, standing a little removed from the three others — holding his alto sax at the ready. Yet something like deer-jacking was in the air of Jersey's little uptown nightclub, intensely white-lighted indicators that the evening was seriously off kilter. Billy was slumped over the old Steinway like he'd had three Singapore slings too many. If you were sitting near the front, in fact, you could have heard Des remark, "Reminds me of the guy who asks, 'Hey, bartender, do you serve zombies?' and the bartender says, 'Sure, what'll you have?'"

What you didn't hear was Billy's usual command before the quartet launched into their big hit, *The Big Band Theory of the Universe*. "Play like hell or I'll kill you," Billy always said, before counting the 5/4 opener in to cheers of recognition. Instead, tonight you would have heard Terry laugh in the dark as the bow from Jimmy's bass moved into the spotlight to nudge Billy, who responded by slumping solemnly towards the audience, banging out a dissonant E-flat minor seventh as his forearm and head slipped off the soundboard onto the Steinway's keyboard. As the house lights came up, Billy toppled head first to the floor, the piano bench slowly tipping the opposite way behind him, then hitting the stage with a decisive bang and spilling Jersey's collection of old *Playboy* magazines from under its lid. Just before Billy fell, you could quite clearly see the drumsticks dangling from his neck — like, Des would later say, "the big old tacky earrings on your average wired streetwalker."

Of course it was his penchant for gallows humour that would help earn Des Cheshire some rather pointed critical attention. And that attention would bring Yours Now and Then Truly, along with my occasionally faithful companion, Theodore E. Mariner, justice of appeal, to Des Cheshire's defence.

How His Lordship and I had ended up at the Chicken Alley at the time in question is a blood-and-guts melodrama in itself. When he was in law school, Justice Mariner had waited table for Jersey at the Alley — waited table, bussed table, swept the floors, cleaned the toilets, mopped the puke, pincered the hypodermics and condoms off the restroom floors with the fry chef's tongs, chauffeured drunken musicians back and forth between their hotels and their gig at the Alley, and intervened in fisticuffs, lover's quarrels and the occasional cat or racoon fight among the garbage cans out back. The budding lawyer had found himself (in other words) on general, all-around clean-up in the down-and-dirty little tavern backing onto the long alleyway off of Cumberland near Bay Street. Then, too, there were the evenings when the band didn't show up at all and, with the patrons getting restless and ready to hot-foot it, the callow law student was invited to show them what he could do at the ivories. Briefs, they called him, not necessarily because his girlfriend of the day had given him boxer shorts with the scales of justice printed on them, but probably because whenever they asked young Ted Mariner what he was doing with his school books spread all over the bar during his breaks he would reply, "The usual, just briefing the cases."

From then on, to fill the musical voids, it was "Hey, Briefs, show us what you can do." And a passable Fats Waller-style barrelhouse was what Briefs Mariner could do, as I can attest at first hand. Nearly forty years later the gift's still more or less with him, along with his razor-sharp ear for the false note in an alibi, honed in the next twenty-odd years of practice at the criminal law bar.

Of course, Briefs Mariner's menial and musical days at the Alley were history long before the white-shoe developers and bomber-jacket impresarios gentrified Yorkville with bistros and steakhouses. At least a decade passed before the little enclave of one-way streets filled with German luxury cars and the after-eight cokeheads who worked in the law firms and stock brokerages a few blocks south. In the old days, Jersey's crowd came by their *delirium tremens* and withdrawal symptoms in the same shirt and tie they had worn the day before, and the day before that, and the week before that, racking their ragged brains for where they could beg, allegedly borrow, or straight-out rip off the cash for their next fix and smoke. "And thank goodness for that," His Lordship is prone to reminisce. "As one of my buddies on the garbage trucks said in those days, 'It might be shit to you, but it's bread and butter to me.' Those junkies, boozehounds, and wiseguys were my bread and butter. They helped me get my practice on its feet — them and their legal aid certificates."

As I have recounted earlier* the judge and I hooked up when the staff at the Great Library of Osgoode Hall, seat of the province's Law Society and highest courts, rescued me, in their humble opinion, from the streets of downtown Toronto. No, I was not one of the homeless and needy who wander into the soup kitchen in the Hall's basement cafeteria several days a week, to avail themselves of the Law Society's Out of the Cold program. Indeed I am not even human or *Homo allegedly sapiens* — H.A.S. for short, or "Has-beings" as they are known among my own kind. As those of you previously acquainted with my legal adventures will recall, I am of the Bar of *felis sylvestris*, laterally known as *felis catus* or, yes, a completely independent and self-reliant C-A-T for short. And I am congenitally equipped for life at the law courts, as though nature had fore-ordained it, all in my robe of silken black fur, with the two white stripes running down my neck at a forty-five degree angle one to the other, just like the tabs the barristers wear over their black gowns in Osgoode Hall's courtrooms. And so, although I am not always popular with the habitués of the Hall, they have dubbed me Amicus, for *amicus curiae*, of course, friend of the court — or, in full, Amicus, Q.C., for Questing Cat, and your Quintessential Correspondent.

During the second year of my acquaintance with the judge,

* See *Murder at Osgoode Hall*, 2004.

domestic strife entered life *chez* Mariner. His Lordship blames it on Mrs. Mariner's menopausal hormones. Penny (so Mrs. Mariner is called by her familiars) blames it primarily on His Lordship's choice of new law clerks, the otherwise highly recommended Nadia Hussein, second in her graduating class at Osgoode Hall Law School.

Nadia was somewhat younger than both Mariner daughters, the ethereal Claire, who recently had become a mother and was on leave as second-chair oboist with the Calgary Symphony Orchestra, and the more urbane Catherine, who was a chip off the old block but with polish — a high-flying corporate lawyer at a large and prestigious law firm on Bay Street. The upshot was that after the gardening and the cooking and the book club and the volunteer work at the Canadian Opera Company were seen to, Mrs. Mariner — Penny — was at a loose end. Meanwhile, and I can vouch for this, His Lordship had begun spending even more hours at the office (judge's chambers these days, of course) than previously had been his habit in his many very busy years at the bar. Whether this was due to the fact that Penny suddenly had more time and inclination to pass judgment on His Lordship's conduct and character I cannot say for sure. Her view on things in general these days certainly was at least occasionally informed by hot flashes and mood swings, as she herself admitted. "I feel like one of those dying stars," I once heard the poor woman say in mid flash, "going out with a whimper, her banging days being well and truly behind her." I believe she and one of the female judges were sharing mid-life war stories at the time, during some drinkie-poos and two-bite quiche function at Osgoode Hall. In any case, Penny Mariner lately had come to feel that, after three decades, His

Lordship had given more of himself than was necessary to his profession and public service, and it was time to balance out the ledger as paterfamilias and new granddad.

Truth to tell, His Lordship had chosen an unusually attractive young woman for this year's clerk. I will leave it to you as jurors, my readers, to decide on the evidence in what follows if the judge's choice of Nadia Hussein was a symptom of a mid-life crisis of his own (as Penny Mariner seemed to think), perhaps complementing, or in reaction to, his wife's passage across the threshold of menopause. Let it be said immediately, however, that if Nadia Hussein was a floozy, as far as I could tell she had little opportunity to practice that avocation. While the judge took her for the occasional lunch or drink, pending further investigation I must say that she was otherwise totally pre-occupied with research for His Lordship and the other appeal judges. And as you will see, she was a great deal more than an exotically pretty face. So all I can state for sure is that push inevitably came to shove, and, having jammed the contents of His Lordship's dresser into an old duffel bag — probably from the judge's law school days, in fact — Penny Mariner queried (as we say over at the Court of Appeal): "You like it in chambers with your floozy night and day, day and night? Why bother to come home, then?"

As for me, well, my billet at the library had received one sniffy complaint too many from alleged allergy sufferers, and there was a similar problem *chez* Mariner. Mrs. His Lordship, a.k.a. the tarnished Penny, wouldn't have me in the house on the off-chance that daughter Claire, who was allergic, herself, might want to bring the new baby, who could have inherited said allergy to feline dander. "I'm not taking the chance," Penny adamantly said one evening ante-bust-up, as His Lordship stood at the front door of their Upper Forest Hill abode, holding Yours Waifishly in the Humpty Dumpty potato chip carton the librarians had cut down for my bed. I fetchingly and vulnerably showed my belly, taking great pains to look absurdly unthreatening on the old blanket in the box. But it was to no avail.

Bailiff, take the prisoners down to the cells!

Of course, just like His Lordship, my record of previous convictions totted up against me: first-degree aviacide on the Hall's front lawn (I harvested a male cardinal whose love life with its mate His Lordship had closely followed from chambers); vandalizing (in said chambers) the upholstery on an antique chair, formerly owned by John Beverley Robinson, 1791 to 1863, Attorney General and Chief Justice of Upper Canada for 33 years; recklessly or negligently or with undue regard for public safety tripping the current Chief Justice on the main staircase to the first floor; going AWOL when in custody in other domestic arrangements; and similar, absolutely natural proclivities which the unjust Has-being considers criminal activity when engaged in by any other species.

Talk about giving a dog a bad name. Or, as His Lordship sums me up in one of his lamer attempts at humour: "His picture's next to the definitions for both 'mischief' and 'nuisance,' you know, in *Black's Law Dictionary*."

Assistant Librarian Katrina Slovenskaya, my official guardian at the library (and my official rescuer from death row in the Doghouse — the humane society shelter on River Street), had two cats of her own at home. So taking me in was out of the question for her good self. Probably I could have dossed down with one of the other librarians, or perhaps with someone working in the Law Society's education wing. But suddenly there was the judge alone and lonely after 31 years of cohabitation with the old Penny. How could I leave the ancient Mariner to fend for himself, after he had provided safe harbour to Yours More or Less Truly at Osgoode Hall?

I wouldn't go so far as to say that Jersey was understanding about our homelessness. However, after muttering and hemming and hawing and looking at his freshly mopped floor a few times (which had me woozy and teetering on all fours in the stench of bleach), he agreed that we could stay upstairs at the Alley for a little while, he supposed, especially seeing how we were offering to pay him a hundred bucks a week cash for his trouble — a C-note, off the books, to sleep (we'd be lucky) on the torn-up old hide-a-bed couch that had been there since before His Lordship's law school days.

"Mind you don't be running up any kind of tab or nothing like that, neither, son."

Son. At fifty-something. "Wouldn't think of abusing your hospitality, Jers," we responded.

"And I suppose you'll be wanting to keep that critter in here with you." At this, Jersey nudged Yours Nearly Asphyxiated with his boot.

"Please," His Lordship replied, looking all apologetic like some big, soft kid. "He's not really such a bad old sidekick. And he'll keep your mice and cockroaches down to a dull roar."

Jersey threw him one of his trademarked bloodshot stares and said: "You telling me I got vermins in my bar, Briefs?"

His Lordship looked at the floor, scuffing his shoes. "Joke, Jers, just a joke. I'm just saying, you know, if you *did* . . ."

"He make any kind of a mess, the both of youse is out of here like a shot, just after y'all reimburses me for whatever he done. Fact, I'll be seeing your first month's rent up front as a damage deposit before I give y'all the key. That's the law, you know, Briefs."

Apparently nobody in the joint had heard of the presumption of innocence. His Lordship wrote a cheque.

"Hey, and Briefs?" Jersey said, inspecting the cheque closely between his sixteen-ounce sirloin hands.

"Yeah, Jers."

"I ain't got no vermins in my place. You dig?"

"Of course you don't, Jersey. No one knows that better than your old mop-boy. Clean as a whistle, or at least an alto sax."

Jersey shook his head. "Everybody's a comedian around my place." He gave us another look of disgust, which grew darker each hour that His Lordship spent in front of the television set above the bar during the next couple of weeks, seeking counsel from Judge Judy, Doctor Phil, and the queen of them all, Miss Oprah Winfrey.